In the Line of Battle

Soldiers' Stories of the War

Walter Wood

In the Line of Battle: Soldiers' Stories of the War

ISBN: 978-1-64799-171-5

INTRODUCTION

The narratives in this volume, which is a companion to my Soldiers' Stories of the War, are told on exactly the same lines as those which were adopted for that collection. There was a personal interview to get the teller's own tale; then the writing, the object being to act as the soldier's other self; and finally the submission to him of the typescript, so that he could revise and become responsible for the completed work.

In dealing with these records I have tried to be a faithful interpreter or reproducer of a tale that has been told to me. I have invited a man to tell his story as it came into his mind, and to look upon me simply as a means of putting it into concrete and coherent form, and as a medium between himself and the reader. The greatest difficulty that had to be overcome was a narrator's reluctance to speak of his own achievements, though he never failed to wax enthusiastic when telling of the doings of his comrades. Nothing has left a deeper impression on my mind than the generous praise which a gunner, say, has bestowed upon the infantry, and the blessings that the infantry have invoked upon the gunners. Never in any of Great Britain's wars has there been such an exhibition of universal esprit de corps as we have witnessed in this stupendous conflict between civilisation and freedom and cultured barbarism and tyranny.

Nothing could have been more encouraging to me as compiler and editor of these true tales than the generous praise that was given to the companion volume. I am grateful to all my critics, who, without exception, so far as I know, welcomed and accepted the work for what it professed to be—an honest contribution on behalf of soldiers to the history of the war.

I set out to do a certain thing—to act as pilot to members of a wondrous band who found themselves in unknown waters, and I succeeded past my utmost expectations. I am proud to think that any act of mine has put on record the doings of patriotic men who have fought so nobly for their country; and thankful to feel that I have been the means of getting for his relatives and friends and all the rest of us the experiences of more than one fine fellow who since I saw him has answered the roll-call for the last time.

Walter Wood

CONTENTS

Introduction iii

CHAPTER I   How Trooper Potts won the V.C. on Burnt Hill
Trooper Frederick William Owen Potts, 1/1st Berkshire Yeomanry (T.F.). 1

CHAPTER II   A Prisoner of War in Germany Corporal Oliver H. Blaze, 1st Battalion Scots Guards. 11

CHAPTER III   Gassed near Hill 60
Lance-Corporal R. G. Simmins, 8th Battalion Canadian Infantry, 90th Winnipeg Rifles. 21

CHAPTER IV   A Linesman in Gallipoli
Private John Frank Gray, 5th Battalion Wiltshire Regiment. 28

CHAPTER V   An Anzac's Adventures
Trooper Rupert Henderson, 6th Australian Light Horse. 39

CHAPTER VI   "Imperishable Glory" for the Kensingtons
—, 13th (Kensington) Battalion London Regiment. 50

CHAPTER VII   Ten Months in the Fighting-Line Private Frederick Woods, 1st Battalion Royal Irish Fusiliers. 59

CHAPTER VIII   A Gunner at the Dardanelles
Gunner John Evans, 92nd Battery Royal Field Artillery. 71

CHAPTER IX   The "Flood"
Corporal Guy Silk, 2nd Battalion Royal Fusiliers. 81

CHAPTER X   The Belgians' Fight with German Hosts
                   Soldat François Rombouts, 8th Regiment
                   of the Line, Belgian Army. 83

CHAPTER XI   A Blinded Prisoner of the Turks Private
                   David Melling, 1/8th Battalion Lancashire
                   Fusiliers. 93

CHAPTER XII   How the "Formidable" was Lost William
                   Edward Francis, Stoker. 100

CHAPTER XIII   A Trooper's Tale
                   Trooper Notley, 5th Dragoon Guards. 107

CHAPTER XIV   A Diarist under Fire
                   Private Charles Hills, 2nd Battalion
                   Australian Infantry. 113

CHAPTER XV   A Stretcher-Bearer at Loos
                   Private Harold Edwards, D.C.M., 1st
                   Battalion South Staffordshire Regiment. . 123

CHAPTER XVI   A Fusilier in France
                     Private Fred. Knott, Royal Fusiliers. 129

CHAPTER XVII   The Daily Round
                   A Subaltern's Diary. 136

CHAPTER XVIII   Saving the Soldier
                   Dr. Wilfred T. Grenfell, C.M.G. 146

CHAPTER I

HOW TROOPER POTTS WON THE V.C. ON BURNT HILL

[As part of the operations in Gallipoli, it was decided to bombard and attack a very strongly fortified Turkish position near Suvla Bay—a sector stretching from Hill 70 to Hill 112. The frontal attack was a desperate enterprise, as the Turks had dug themselves in up to the neck in two lines of trenches of exceptional strength. The attack was made on the afternoon of August 21st, 1915, after a bombardment by battleships and heavy land batteries. It was in the course of this advance that the teller of this story, Trooper Frederick William Owen Potts, of the 1/1st Berkshire Yeomanry (Territorial Force), was struck down, and later performed the unparalleled act for which he was awarded the Victoria Cross. For nearly fifty hours Trooper Potts remained under the Turkish trenches with a severely wounded and helpless comrade, "although he could himself have returned to safety," says the official record. Finally the trooper, in the extraordinary manner which he now describes, saved his comrade's life. Trooper Potts is only twenty-two years old, and is the first Yeoman to win the most coveted of all distinctions.]

I saw a good deal of the Turks before we came to grips with them near Suvla Bay. I had gone out to Egypt with my regiment, the Berkshire Yeomanry, and for about four months we were doing garrison work and escort work for Turks who had been captured in Gallipoli and the Dardanelles and sent as prisoners of war to Egypt. Our place was not far from Cairo. I was greatly struck by the size and physique of the Turks. There were some very fine big men amongst them—in fact, I should think the average height was close on six feet.

We had taken our horses out to Egypt with us, and all our work in that country was done with them; but as the weeks went by, and no call came to us for active service, we became disappointed, and got into the way of singing a song which the poet of the regiment had specially composed, and of which the finish of every verse was the line—

1

this meaning that there was no use for us as cavalry in the fighting area. But when the four months had gone, the order suddenly came for us to go to Gallipoli. By that time we had got acclimatised, a point we appreciated later, as the heat was intense and the flies were very troublesome.

From Alexandria we sailed in a transport, which occupied four days in reaching Gallipoli. Here we were transhipped to trawlers and barges, and immediately found ourselves in the thick of one of the most tremendous bombardments the world has ever known. Battleships were firing their big guns, which made a terrific noise, and there was other continual firing of every known sort. We were very lucky in our landing, because we escaped some of the heaviest of the gun-fire. The Turks could see us, though we had no sight of them, and whenever a cluster of us was spotted, a shell came crashing over. Thus we had our baptism of fire at the very start.

We were in an extraordinarily difficult country, and whatever we needed in the way of food and drink we had to carry with us— even the water. Immense numbers of tins had been filled from the Nile and taken to Gallipoli in barges, and this was the water we used for drinking purposes, as well as water which was condensed from the sea, and kept in big tanks on the shore. Every drop of water we needed had to be fetched from the shore, and this work proved about the hardest and most dangerous of any we had to do after landing and taking up our position on a hill. Several of our chaps were knocked over in this water-fetching work.

While we were at this place we were employed in making roads from Suvla Bay to Anzac, and hard work it was, because the country was all rocks. We had landed light, without blankets or waterproofs, so that we felt the intense cold of the nights very much.

We had a week of this sort of thing, under fire all the time. I think it was on a Sunday we landed, and a week later we heard that we were to take part in the attack on Hill 70, or, as we called it, because of its appearance, Burnt Hill. There were immense quantities of a horrible sort of scrub on it, and a great deal of this stuff had been fired and charred by gun-fire. I little knew then how close and long an acquaintance I was to make with the scrub on Hill 70.

It was about five o'clock in the evening when the great news came. We were to be ready at seven, and ready we were, glad to be in it. We did not know much, but we understood that we were to take our places in some reserve trenches. Night comes quickly in those regions, and when the day had gone we moved round to

Anzac, marching along the roads which we had partially made. We reached Anzac at about two o'clock in the morning, in pitch darkness.

We had a pick and two shovels to four men, and took it in turn to carry them. Each man also carried two hundred rounds of ammunition, so that we were pretty well laden. When we reached Anzac Cove we moved in right under the cliffs, which go sheer down to the sea; but there is practically no tide, so that the beach is safe. The only way to reach the shore was to go in single file down a narrow, twisting pathway.

We were on the beach till about two o'clock in the afternoon, when we were ordered to be ready with our packs, and we went up the cliff, again in single file, forming up when we reached the top. Then we went a mile or so along the road we had marched over the night before—all part of the scheme of operations, I take it. Then we cut across to our right and saw a plain called Salt Lake, where we watched a division going into action under heavy shrapnel fire.

We were now in the thick of the awful country which I was to know so well. The surface was all sand and shrubs, and the great peculiarity of the shrubs was that they were very much like our holly trees at home, though the leaves were not so big, but far more prickly. These shrubs were about three feet high, and they were everywhere; but they did not provide any real cover. There were also immense numbers of long creepers and grass, and a lot of dust and dirt. The heat was fearful, so that you can easily understand how hard it was to get along when we were on the move. These obstacles proved disastrous to many of our chaps when they got into the zone of fire, for the shrapnel set the shrubs ablaze. This meant that many a brave fellow who was hit during the fighting on Hill 70 fell among the burning furze and was burned to death where he lay.

As we were waiting for our turn, we could see the other chaps picking their way through this burning stuff, and charging on towards the Turkish trenches. When our own turn came, the scrub was burning less fiercely, and to some extent we were able to choose our way and avoid the blazing patches. We ran whenever we got the chance, making short rushes; but when we got into the real zone of fire, we never stopped until we were under the protection of Chocolate Hill.

For half an hour we rested at the foot of this hill. From our position we could not see the Turks, who were entrenched over the top; but their snipers were out and bothering us a good deal. It was impossible to see these snipers, because they hid themselves most cunningly in the bushes, and had their faces and rifles painted the same colour as the surrounding objects. However, we levelled up matters by sending out our own sniping parties.

We were on the move again as soon as we had got our breath back. We still understood, as we moved to the left of Chocolate Hill, that we were going to occupy reserve trenches. We went through a field of ripe wheat. About two yards in front of me was a mate of mine, Reginald West. I saw him struck in the thigh by a sniper's bullet, which went in as big as a pea, and came out the size of a five-shilling piece. It was an explosive bullet, one of many that were used against us by the Turks, under their German masters. In a sense West was lucky, because when he was struck down he fell right on the edge of a dug-out, and I heard one of the men shout, "Roll over, mate! Roll over! You'll drop right in here!" And he did.

The rest of us went on, though in the advance we lost a number of men. Some were killed outright; some were killed by shells and bullets after they had fallen wounded, and some had to lie where they had fallen and do the best they could. We pushed ahead till we struck Hill 70 again.

When we got to the reserve trenches I asked a chap how far away the Turks were, and he answered, "About a thousand yards," but I don't think it was as much as that.

Now we began to ascend Hill 70 in short spurts, halting from time to time. We had fairly good cover, because the scrub was not on fire, though several parts had been burnt out. During one of these halts we were ordered to fix bayonets.

We had found shelter in a bit of a gulley, and were pretty well mixed up with other regiments—the Borders, Dorsets, and so on. We first got the idea that we were going to charge from an officer near us; but he was knocked out—with a broken arm, I believe—before the charge came off. He was just giving us the wheeze about the coming charge when a bullet struck him.

How did the charge begin? Well, an officer shouted, as far as I can recollect, "Come on, lads! We'll give 'em beans!" That is not exactly according to drill-books and regulations as I know them; but it was enough. It let the boys loose, and they simply leapt forward and went for the Turkish trenches. It was not to be my good fortune to get into them, however; in fact, I did not get very far after the order to charge was given.

I had gone perhaps twenty or thirty yards when I was knocked off my feet. I knew I was hit. I had a sort of burning sensation; but whether I was hit in the act of jumping, or whether I jumped because I was hit, I do not know. What I do know is that I went up in the air, came down again, and lay where I fell. I knew that I had been shot at the top of the left thigh, the bullet going clean through

4

and just missing the artery and the groin by an eighth of an inch, as the doctor told me later.

Utterly helpless, I lay there for about three-quarters of an hour, while the boys rushed round me and scattered in the charge. This happened about a quarter of a mile from the top of the hill. I propped myself up on my arm and watched the boys charging.

I heard later, from a man who was with me in hospital at Malta—he had been struck deaf and dumb, for the time being, amongst other things—that the boys got into the Turkish third trench and that the Turks bolted. He told me that when they reached this third trench there were only seventeen Berkshire boys left to hold it. The enemy seemed to get wind of this; then it looked as if all the Turkish army was going for the seventeen, and they had no alternative but to clear out.

After the charge I saw this handful come back down the hill, quite close to where I was lying. I had fallen in a sort of little thicket, a cluster of the awful scrub which was like holly, but much worse. I was thankful for it, however, because it gave me a bit of shelter and hid me from view.

I had been lying there about half an hour when I heard a noise near me and saw that a poor wounded chap, a trooper of the Berkshires, was crawling towards me. I recognised him as a fellow-townsman.

"Is that you, Andrews?" I asked.

He simply answered "Yes." That was all he could get out.

"I'm jolly pleased you've come," I said, and Andrews crawled as close as he could get, and we lay there, perfectly still, for about ten minutes. Andrews had been shot through the groin, a very dangerous wound, and he was suffering terribly and losing a great deal of blood.

We had been together for a few minutes when another trooper—a stranger to me—crawled up to our hiding-place. He had a wound in the leg. We were so cramped for space under the thicket, that Andrews had to shift as best he could, to make room for the newcomer. That simple act of mercy saved his life, for the stranger had not been with us more than ten minutes when a bullet went through both his legs and mortally wounded him. He kept on crying for water; but we had not a drop amongst the three of us, and could not do anything to quench his awful thirst.

That fearful afternoon passed slowly, with its grizzling heat and constant fighting, and the night came quickly. The night hours brought us neither comfort nor security, for a full moon shone, making the countryside as light as day. The cold was intense. The stranger was practically unconscious and kept moving about, which made our position worse, because every time he moved the Turks banged at us.

I was lying absolutely as flat as I could, with my face buried in the dirt, for the bullets were peppering the ground all around us, and one of them actually grazed my left ear—you can see the scar it has made, just over the top. This wound covered my face with blood. Was I scared or frightened? I can honestly say that I was not. I had got beyond that stage, and almost as a matter of course I calmly noted the details of everything that happened.

Throughout the whole of that unspeakable night this poor Bucks Hussar chap hung on. He kept muttering, "Water! Water!" But we could not give him any. When the end came he simply lay down and died right away, and his dead body stayed with us, for we could neither get away nor move him.

During the whole of the next day we lay in our hiding-place, suffering indescribably. The sun, thirst, hunger, and our wounds, all added to our pain. In our desperation we picked bits off the stalks of the shrubs and tried to suck them; but we got no relief in that way.

The whole of the day went somehow—with such slowness that it seemed as if it would never end. It was impossible to sleep—fighting was going on all the time, and the noise was terrific. We could not see anything of our boys, and we knew that it was impossible for any stretcher-bearers to get through to us, because we were a long way up the hill and no stretcher-bearers could venture out under such a terrible fire.

Night came again at last, and Andrews and myself decided to shift, if it was humanly possible to do so, because it was certain death from thirst and hunger to remain where we were, even if we escaped from bullets. So I began to move away by crawling, and Andrews followed as best he could. I would crawl a little way and wait till Andrews, poor fellow, could crawl up to me again. We wriggled like snakes, absolutely flat on the ground and with our faces buried in the stifling dirt.

We managed to wriggle about three hundred yards that night—as near as I can judge. Starting at about a quarter past six, as soon as the day was done, it was about three in the morning when we decided to rest, so that if we had really done three hundred yards we had crawled at the rate of only thirty-three yards an hour!

A great number of rifles were lying about—weapons which had been cast aside in the charge, or had belonged to fallen soldiers; but most of them were quite out of working order, because they were clogged up with dust and dirt. I tried many of them, and at last found one that seemed to be in good working order, and to my joy I came across about fifty rounds of ammunition. Another serviceable rifle was found, so that Andrews and myself were filled with a new hope.

"We'll die like Britons, at any rate!" said Andrews. "We'll give a good account of ourselves before we go!" And I agreed with him.

We were now some distance from the Turks, and I was terribly anxious to shoot at them; but Andrews was more cautious. "If you fire they'll discover us, and we shall be done for!" he said. Then we shook hands fervently, because we both believed that this was the last of us, and I know that in thought we both went back to our very early days and offered up our silent prayers to God.

We had managed to crawl to a bit of shelter which was given by some burnt-out scrub, and here we tried to snatch some sleep, for we were both worn out. We went to sleep, for the simple reason that we could not keep awake; but I suddenly awoke, because the cold was intense and I was nearly frozen. Luckily there were a lot of empty sandbags lying about, and I got two or three of these and put them on top of us; but they were really no protection from the bitter air.

When the morning came we made a move, and for the first time we were able to get some water; but only by taking the water-bottles from the poor chaps who had been knocked out.

Then we crept back to our shelter, finding immense relief from drinking the water we had got, though it was quite warm and was, I fancy, from the Nile.

We slept, or tried to sleep, there for the rest of that night, and stayed in the place till next morning. We must have been in what is called "dead ground," a region which cannot be seen or touched by either side, and so it proved to be, for in the early morning there was a real battle and the bullets were singing right over our heads.

"There's more lead flying about than there was yesterday," said Andrews; and really some of the bullets were splashing quite close to us—within six feet, I think, though there were not many that came so near.

Andrews was bleeding terribly—every time he moved he bled; but I did the best I could for him with my iodine—I dressed him with mine, and he dressed me with his, and splendid stuff it is. Though we had nothing to eat we did not really feel hungry now— we were past the eating stage. I was very lucky in having four cigarettes and some matches and I risked a smoke, the sweetest I ever had in my life.

Again we stuck the awful day through.

I was terribly anxious to move and get out of it all at any cost; but still Andrews was very cautious. "No, we won't try till it gets dark," he said. I felt that he was right, and so we waited, as patiently as we could, for the night. Three or four yards from us was an inviting-looking bush, and we crawled towards it, thinking it would help us to get away and give us shelter; but at the end of our adventure we discovered that we had done no more than crawl to the bush, crawl round it, and get back to our original hiding-place; so we decided to give up the attempt to get away just then.

When the third night on the hill came we were fairly desperate, knowing that something would have to be done if we meant to live, and that certain death awaited us where we were. We had nothing to eat, and the only drink was the water, which was frightful stuff—I believe it was Nile water which had been brought. But though it was, we were thankful to have it. The water was warm, because of the heat, and was about the colour of wine.

We did not for a moment suppose that we should live to reach the British lines, which we believed to be not far away; but we risked everything on the effort, and in the moonlight we began to wriggle off. We had managed to get no more than half a dozen yards when Andrews had to give it up. I myself, though I was the stronger and better of the two, could scarcely crawl. Every movement was a torture and a misery, because of the thorns that stuck into us from the horrible scrub.

We had kept the sandbags, and with my help Andrews managed to get them over his arms and up to his shoulders. I fastened them with the pieces of string they have, and these gave him a good deal of protection, though the thorns got through and punished us cruelly. I was picking them out of my hands for three weeks afterwards.

Having crawled these half-dozen yards, we gave up the attempt altogether, and did not know what to do. We could see a cluster of trees not far away, about a hundred yards, and there was one that looked fairly tall.

"If we can get to that tree," said Andrews, "I could lie there, if I had some water, and perhaps you could strike some of our chaps and bring help." I had little hope from such an effort as that. Then Andrews unselfishly urged me to look after myself; but, of course, I would not dream of leaving him. I offered to carry him, and I tried, but I was far too weak.

What in the world was to be done? How were we to get out of this deadly place? There seemed no earthly hope of escape, when, literally like an inspiration, we thought we saw a way out.

Just near us was an ordinary entrenching shovel, which had been dropped, or had belonged to some poor chap who had fallen—I can't say which, but there it was. I crawled up and got hold of it, and before we quite knew what was happening, Andrews was resting on it, and I was doing my best to drag him out of danger.

I cannot say whose idea this was, but it is quite likely that Andrews thought of it first. He sat on the shovel as best he could—he was not fastened to it—with his legs crossed, the wounded leg over the sound one, and he put his hands back and clasped my wrists as I sat on the ground behind and hauled away at the handle. Several times he came off, or the shovel fetched away, and I soon saw that it would be impossible to get him away in this fashion.

When we began to move the Turks opened fire on us; but I hardly cared now about the risk of being shot, and for the first time since I had been wounded I stood up and dragged desperately at the shovel, with Andrews on it. I managed to get over half a dozen yards, then I was forced to lie down and rest. Andrews needed a rest just as badly as I did, for he was utterly shaken and suffered greatly.

We started again at about a quarter past six, as soon as the night came, and for more than three mortal hours we made this strange journey down the hillside; and at last, with real thankfulness, we reached the bottom and came to a bit of a wood. Sweet beyond expression it was to feel that I could walk upright, and that I was near the British lines. This knowledge came to me suddenly when there rang through the night the command: "Halt!"

I obeyed—glorious it was to hear that challenge in my native tongue, after what we had gone through. Then this good English sentry said, "Come up and be recognised!" not quite according to the regulation challenge, but good enough—and he had seen us quite clearly in the moonshine.

Up I went, and found myself face to face with the sentry, whose rifle was presented ready for use, and whose bayonet gleamed in the cold light.

"What are you doing?" said the sentry. "Are you burying the dead?"

I saw that he was sentry over a trench, and I went to the top of it and leaned over the parapet and said, "Can you give me a hand?"

"What's up?" said the sentry, who did not seem to realise what had actually happened—and how could he, in such a strange affair?

"I've got a chap out here wounded," I told him, "and I've dragged him down the hill on a shovel."

The sentry seemed to understand like a flash. He walked up to the trench, and when I had made myself clear, three or four chaps bustled round and got a blanket, and I led them to the spot where I had left Andrews lying on the ground. We lifted him off the shovel, put him on the blanket, and carried him to the trench. These men were, I think, Inniskilling Fusiliers, and they did everything for us that human kindness could suggest. They gave me some rum and bully beef and biscuit, and it was about the most delightful meal I ever had in my life, because I was famishing and I was safe, with Andrews, after those dreadful hours on the hillside, which seemed as if they would never end.

When we had rested and pulled round a bit, we were put on stretchers and carried to the nearest dressing-station. Afterwards we were sent to Malta, where Andrews is, I believe, still in hospital.

The granting of the Victoria Cross for what I had done came as a complete surprise to me, because it never struck me that I had done more than any other British soldier would have done for a comrade.

I never lost heart during the time I was lying on Hill 70. All the old things came clearly up in my mind, and many an old prayer was uttered, Andrews joining in. We never lost hope that some way out of our peril would be found—and it seemed as if our prayers had been answered by giving us this inspiration of the shovel.

CHAPTER II

A PRISONER OF WAR IN GERMANY

[For nine weary months, including the whole of an uncommonly bitter winter, the teller of this story, Corporal Oliver H. Blaze, 1st Battalion Scots Guards, was a prisoner of war in Germany. Corporal Blaze was on outpost when he was severely wounded and captured, and his subsequent experiences give proof that in this momentous struggle we are fighting a people who are incapable of understanding the laws of honourable combat, and who, in the interests of humanity and civilisation, must be crushed. Corporal Blaze is a fine type of the splendid Guardsmen who have done so much in this great war to add to their own glory and the noble reputation of the British Army.]

I hardly know where to begin my story, but perhaps I might start with a little tale of an air fight, because a night or two ago I happened to be in the streets when German airships raided London, and I could not help recalling the difficulty of hitting even a huge object like a Zeppelin in the night-time.

In the early days of September 1914, when we had got used to fighting, the battalion was on the march when a German aeroplane, decorated with two Iron Crosses, was sighted. At that time we were more than a thousand strong, and the lot of us opened fire with our rifles, rattling away with rapid fire, so that we soon accounted for about fifteen thousand rounds. At the same time another battalion not far away was on the job, so that a perfect fusillade was going on. The firing was tremendous, but it seemed as if the machine would not be touched. At last, however, the aeroplane was brought down, the observer being dead and the other man severely burnt and wounded. I do not know whether it was our battalion or the other which got the machine; but I called to mind the great difficulty of hitting an aircraft when I watched the raid on London. I was walking along, too pleasantly occupied to be thinking of war, and did not know of the affair until I reached a street corner and saw the people craning their necks skywards, watching the airship and the shells that were bursting under it.

Mons, Cambrai, the Marne and the like make an old, old story by this time, so I will get on to the tale of my nine months' captivity in Germany, as a prisoner of war.

It is common knowledge now that the Germans never lost a chance of trying to do something by treachery and trickery and not playing the game. Killed and wounded English soldiers were robbed of their coats by the Germans, who took them for their own use; and dressed in these coats the enemy on several occasions tried to get near us, to their heavy cost, when we got accustomed to the dodge.

One day, early in September, not long after we had gone out with the Expeditionary Force, a German machine-gun brigade came along, dressed in our uniform. We thought they were reinforcements, so we let them get very close and they occupied a ridge on our left. Ten minutes afterwards they opened fire on us; but our garrison artillery soon shifted them with sixty-pounders. The Germans killed a lot of the Coldstreams that day by this trick.

It was not long after this that we had one of those experiences which have been so often known in this great war. We were marching along in brigade column, with the Black Watch or Coldstreams, I am not sure which, leading. We were going through an area which had been reported all clear, and had got to a bend in the road, when the Germans started shelling us. It was one of those swift happenings which cannot be avoided in such a war as this, and before we fully realised what was taking place, a shell had burst and killed four stretcher-bearers of the Coldstreams, the N.C.O. who was in charge, and a wounded man who was being carried on a stretcher; and the same shell wounded a man in our front section of fours. That one shell did a fair lot of havoc, and it was quickly followed by several more; but these did not do much mischief.

What struck me most in this little affair was the coolness of our C.O., Colonel Lowther, now a brigadier-general. He personally conducted every company from the left of the road into a ditch on the right of the road.

"Keep cool, men," he said, "and come this way." And we did keep cool, for the colonel took the direction of everything, in spite of the shelling, just as calmly as if he was carrying out a battalion parade at home—a really wonderful performance at a time like that, and one which completely steadied the lot of us, though we had got pretty well used to things.

But the Germans did not have a look in for long, for the Kilties got hold of the gunners and chased them off. I did not see much of it, except in the distance; but we heard the shouting as the Jocks got to work with their bayonets.

As we were going along the road we saw where the Germans had put out of action a whole battery of our artillery which was standing at the side of the road. The weather was dull and it started to drizzle, so that it was not easy to distinguish troops. While the battery was being knocked out some of our fellows—the Loyal North Lancashire, I think—were advancing across a field. To protect themselves from the rain they had covered themselves with their waterproof sheets. Seeing them, and not being able to tell who they were, but believing them to be Germans, our gunners opened fire on them; but what damage they did I don't know. That was another of those things that will happen in war, and it could hardly be helped, for about this time it was a common dodge of the Germans to disguise themselves in British uniforms and attack us before we could tumble to the trick.

When we had crossed the Aisne and had got into the hills we had grown wary, and in crossing fields and open spaces we went in artillery formation, or "blobbing," as it is called. This "blobbing" was a splendid way of saving the lives of men when we were under fire, for it kept us in platoons closed, but 200 yards between each platoon, and so enabled us to escape a good many of the bursting shells.

We went along a whole stretch of country till we reached a small village and billeted there. In the morning we were on the move again, driving the Germans from one crest to another, but their position was too strong for us to shift them any farther, and then it was a long monotonous job of hanging on and waiting. They are practically in the same place now.

We did a lot of bayonet work from time to time; but I can't say much about it. I know that in one affair I saw a German. I stuck and he stuck—and I don't remember any more—one goes insane. I got a bang on the back of the head from somebody, though I thought at the time that a stone had been thrown and had struck me. I remember that day well—September 14th—because in addition to the charge I saw a Jack Johnson for the first time, though we christened them Black Marias and Coal-boxes then. This monster burst amongst some French Algerian troops, and shot a lot of them up into the air, literally blowing the poor devils to pieces.

On October 19th we marched away and moved by train, finally getting to Ypres. We dug trenches in a ditch on the night of the 22nd and occupied them, and on the morning of the 23rd I went on outpost duty, little dreaming of the fate that was in store for me. At that time shells were dropping very heavily between our line of trenches and a village not far away which was supposed to be occupied by the French.

It was about six o'clock in the morning when I went out with my patrol, of which I was corporal in charge. There were four of us altogether, and we were put on outpost duty in what proved to be a very warm corner. The shelling went on all day, and we were looking forward to our relief; but it did not happen to come, and so we had to hold on. The day passed and the night came, and it was not long after darkness that we knew that a strong rush was being made on us by the enemy—they proved to be the 213th Landwehr Battalion of Prussian Infantry.

I saw that we were being rushed, and I knew that our chance of escape was hopeless. I thought very swiftly just then, and my thought was, "We can't get away, so we may as well stick it. If we bolt we shall be shot in the back—and we might just as well be shot in the front; it looks better."

They were on us before we knew where we were, and to make matters worse, they rushed upon us from the direction of the village where we supposed the French to be.

There was a scrap, short and sweet, between our outpost and the Germans, and almost in the twinkling of an eye, it seemed, two of my men were killed, one got away, and I was wounded and captured.

A bullet struck me in the right arm and I fell down, and the Germans were on me before I knew what was happening. I still had my equipment on, and to this fact and the prompt kind act of a wounded German—let us be fair and say that not all Germans are brutes: there are a few exceptions—I owe my life, for as soon as I fell a Prussian rushed at me and made a drive with his bayonet. Just as he did so, a wounded German who was lying on the ground near me grabbed me and gave me a lug towards him. At this instant the bayonet jabbed at me and struck between the equipment and my wounded arm, just touching my side. The equipment and the wounded German's pull had prevented the bayonet from plunging plump into me and killing me on the spot, for the steel, driven with such force, would have gone clean through my chest. That was the sort of tonic to buck you up, and I didn't need a second prick to make me spring to my feet.

I jumped up, and had no sooner done so than a second bullet struck me on the wounded arm and made a fair mess of it, and I knew that this time I was properly bowled out.

I had fallen down again and was lying on the ground, bleeding badly; and the next thing I knew was that I was being stripped. Everything I had on me, my equipment and my clothing, was taken away; not for the purpose of letting a doctor examine me, as one did later, but as part of a system of battlefield plunder which the Germans have organised.

The very first thing the doctor said when he saw the wounds

was "Donnerwetter!" I was taken to a barn and left there till morning. I had treatment, then I was moved into another barn. The Germans were decent over the business, and there was no brutality or anything of that kind. I had been taken from the second barn, and was being carried across a field, when the ambulance was stopped by a German doctor who was on horseback. He looked at my arm, and instantly said that it would have to be amputated right away, as mortification had set in; and so, lying on the stretcher, which had been put down in the field, and round which a small green tarpaulin had been rigged to keep the wind and cold out, my arm was taken off. Injections had been made in the arm, and I felt no pain during the operation, which I watched with great interest. The doctor who performed it had studied at Guy's Hospital and spoke English well. When I had been removed to a German hospital in Belgium he saw me every morning, noon, and night, and I had exactly the same food as the Germans, while the old inspector of the hospital used to give me custard and fruit now and again, when he thought no one was looking; and I had cigarettes and cigars issued to me just the same as to their own men.

I was in this hospital in Belgium for a fortnight, and was then moved into Germany, being sent to Münster, in Westphalia, with a lot of wounded Germans. It seemed as if, in leaving Belgium, I had said good-bye to civilisation, in view of what happened during my imprisonment in Germany.

I very soon made acquaintance with German brutality to British prisoners of war—brutality and cowardice, of which I saw constant signs in my captivity; I say cowardice advisedly, because only a coward will hit and bully a man who can't hit back. On that point, however, there is some consolation. It was practically a death matter to strike a German soldier, even under great provocation; but if you were struck first, you had your remedy, and nothing pleased a British soldier more than to be struck, because that gave him his chance, and many a hard British fist got home on a fat German jowl. I shall always be thankful to know that I got one or two in on my own account, though I had only my left arm to work with. I did not, of course, strike until I had been struck first; but when I did hit out I got my own back, with a lot of interest.

That is getting off the track a bit, so I will go back. At Münster I was taken into a disused circus which had been turned into a hospital for prisoners, and when I got there the doctor examined my wound. It was all raw, but he messed about to that extent that I fainted. Two mornings afterwards—they only dressed us every two mornings—I was lying on a table, to be dressed. The job was to be done by a young German student, a born brute, for I tell only the

15

plain truth when I say that he deliberately cut the flesh of my only arm with his lancet and scissors.

"English swine!" he said. "He's had one arm off, and he ought to have the other off, too!"

This was the type of fellow who was let loose on wounded helpless British prisoners of war.

Those dressings were horrible experiences, as a rule, for I was held down on the table by German orderlies, who had about as much feeling and compassion as the table itself.

Let me give another illustration of the German way of treating wounded British soldiers. Just after Christmas I was moved into an open camp at Münster, and the only covering I had was a tarpaulin, the result being that I caught cold in my wound, and on January 2nd I was moved back into another hospital. I knew nothing whatever about the regulations of the place, so that I saw nothing wrong in walking along an ordinary looking passage. As I did this there came towards me a man who corresponds in rank to our regimental sergeant-major. I was suffering greatly from my stump, and was quite helpless; yet this fellow seized me by the scruff of the neck and the seat of the trousers and threw me out of the passage—and it was not till later that I learned that the passage led to the operating-room, and that patients were not allowed to use it. Such a thing could not possibly happen in a British military hospital containing wounded German soldiers. It is only fair to say that the food we got in hospital was good.

Though my wound was not healed, I was sent away from the hospital and back to the camp. That was bad in some ways, but it had a fine compensation, for I was attended by two of our own medical officers of the Royal Army Medical Corps who were also prisoners—Captain Rose and Captain Croker. I believe they have been exchanged now. I need not say what a joy it was to be looked after by our own splendid doctors, after my experience of German brutality and callousness.

Time passed slowly and very wearily, and the monotony became deadly. It was bitterly cold, and snow fell heavily and constantly till about April. We did our best to keep cheerful and fit, and were always thankful when we could get a chance of playing games. Sometimes we played football with our sentries; but they were sorry sportsmen, and could not endure being beaten, even in fair football. There were some Royal Welsh Fusiliers amongst the prisoners, and three footballs had been sent out to them. These footballs reached the camp safely, and everybody was hugely pleased with them. We got up a match between a British team and the German sentries, and beat them six to one. It was a straightforward, honest match, and a fair and square win; but the Germans could not stomach it, and for three days our smoking was stopped. No reason for the stoppage was given; but we knew well enough what the cause was, especially as the order applied only to the British prisoners of war.

I will give another instance of the utter smallness of the German spirit. On the night of the day when Italy declared war on Austria we were sitting outside our wooden huts singing our own National Anthem, the "Marseillaise," "Rule, Britannia," and lighter compositions such as "Hi! Tiddley hi ti!"—in fact, anything that came to mind, just to keep things moving and cheerful. Then the news of Italy's decision came and fairly struck the Germans dumb. No reason was given for the steps they took against us—though we knew perfectly well what the cause was—but our smoking was stopped for seven days. Some of us were locked in the lavatories for twenty-four hours, and for twenty days our meat was stopped, so that we were almost starved. And on top of all this, two Englishmen and a Belgian were sent to a punishment camp. God knows what happened to them.

During all this bitter winter weather we were accommodated in wooden huts, which we had been put to build ourselves. We did not mind that in the least, because we were thankful to be employed. But it was almost impossible to keep warm in the huts, owing to our scanty clothing and the small number of stoves. There were two stoves in each room, but we were only allowed one small box of coal—sometimes coke—daily for each. Generally speaking, the British prisoners could not get near the stoves because of the foreign prisoners who crowded around them, all day long, swathed in a pair of blankets. To add to the misery of the life, the bedding was horribly verminous, and we were only allowed to have one wash a day. That solitary wash was early in the morning, and we could not get any more, because the wash-house was closed after 7 a.m.

The food was very poor, and there was not enough of it. There was plenty of soup of a sort—and well there might be, for it was mostly water—and there were solids of a kind for which an Englishman has no liking—chestnuts, potatoes and horse beans—poor stuff after the splendid rations we had had as British soldiers from our own Army Service Corps. The drinks were as bad as the solids. We had what was called coffee given to us; but there was not much difference between the coffee and the soup. As for clothing, no real attempt was made to supply us, though in so many cases we had been stripped naked when captured. When I went out of camp, just after Christmas, I had only a pair of trousers and a pair of sabots, wooden shoes, and I should have fared badly if I had not been lucky enough to receive an old cycling jacket which my mother had sent out to me.

The following statement will show exactly how and when we were fed each day:—In the morning, at six o'clock, we had "coffee," made from burnt rye, but nothing to eat; at twelve noon, soup, with a plentiful supply of water in it and any one of the following ingredients: chestnuts, potatoes, horse beans, sauerkraut, acorns. At 12.30 to 1 p.m. there was an issue of bread, the loaves being about 2½ in. by 6 in. by 2 in. At 3 p.m. there was "coffee," as at 6 a.m., but nothing to eat; and at 6 p.m. there was soup, as for dinner, but no meat, fish or cheese. By this you will see that we had nothing to eat from 6 p.m. till noon the following day—a period of eighteen hours. We had a small piece of meat three times a fortnight, cheese once a week, and two raw herrings a week.

As for passing the time, it was one long dreary "roll on, night." Cards, draughts, football, and causing as much trouble as we dared to the Germans, with a little singing, formed our only means of keeping sane. Nearly everybody had to work at something or other, the hours of work being 7 a.m. to 11.30 a.m. (empty stomachs), and 2 p.m. to 6 p.m.

There was only one occasion when we had a little[change from the bad treatment, and that was when a batch of German prisoners of war, who had been in England and exchanged, returned. They must have told how splendidly they were treated in English hospitals—which, as I know, are paradise compared with German hospitals—for we were better fed and looked after for a time. This improvement did not last long, however, and we went back to the old ways. Germans can't keep a good thing going.

German cunning and lying soon made themselves evident, for under the guise of voluntary work a lot of the prisoners of war were obliged to work in mines and ironworks, and by being forced to do these things they were really helping to fight their own people.

The way the trick was done was this—Germans came round and asked prisoners to volunteer to act as waiters, and a lot of us readily agreed, because any sort of employment was better than awful idleness. But the "waiters" soon learned that they had been shamefully deceived, for they were sent into mines and ironworks and on to farms. It was no use to protest, because it was a case of work or no food. There was so little to eat in the ordinary way that poor fellows could not face actual starvation, and so they worked unwillingly. I was asked to go and work in the fields, but I was quite incapable of doing this, and so I told the camp commandant, who put me into the office.

I had had experience of orderly-room work with the Guards,

18

and felt quite at home at this job—and it was interesting, too, for I was in the extraordinary position of being a sort of censor!

My duty was to handle letters from England for the prisoners, and see that no news, or cuttings from newspapers, or other forbidden things got through. There were three of us doing this work—two sergeants and myself, one sergeant being in charge of the parcels. I naturally did the best I could for the prisoners. This office work was both interesting and exciting, and helped to get the time along.

As for our privations generally, there was nothing for it but to make the best of them and grin and bear it. The American Consul at Münster paid two visits to the camp while I was there, but no good came of them. Again the crafty German was prepared. It was known on each occasion that the Consul was coming—known two days before he arrived—so things were ready for him. He inspected only a few of the rooms, and the principal result of the first visit was that our dinner was two hours late. We made complaints, but nothing came of them, so when the Consul visited us for the second time and asked if there were any complaints to make, we bluntly answered, "No, it's no good making them, for nothing's done." The Germans instantly published in the local paper the statement, "The English are satisfied. They have no complaints."

Constant attempts were made to escape, and I fancy that some of the prisoners gave up the whole of their time to plotting and planning ways of clearing out. The chance of getting away was small, because at night the camp, buildings as well as compounds, was brilliantly lighted by big electric arc lamps, and there were sentries and barbed wire entanglements everywhere. But in spite of all precautions several Belgians and a few Englishmen and Frenchmen escaped, and we were immensely pleased when we heard that one Belgian had got away by stealing the commandant's motor-car and bolting in it. I did not hear what became of him.

Brutal punishments were inflicted for the most trivial offences, such as smoking in forbidden places, and a common method was to tie a prisoner to a post, with his feet deep in snow, and leave him there for two hours, with an armed sentry over him. The poor wretch dare not move, if he did the brave warrior with the gun kicked him—the German is a fine hand at hitting when the other chap can't hit back. This savage cruelty had a terrible effect on some of the victims, and helped to make them the life-long wrecks that they now are.

From Münster I was sent to Brussels for exchange. We were quartered in the Royal Academy, and naturally enough the Belgian women and children tried to give us things. When this was seen, the German wounded who were in the building were ordered to turn the hose on, and they did. It was a great laugh, though, for it took them four hours to fix the hose—and then it would not work properly.

The authorities suddenly decided that I should not be exchanged, because I was a non-commissioned officer, and I was sent to Wesel on the Rhine, where I stayed six weeks. I had to go into hospital again, because my wound would not heal—it never got a sporting chance. Ill treatment continued, and for reasons, mostly revenge, which Britishers would scorn. The chief of this hospital was an old man whose only son had been lost in a submarine that had been sunk by the British. I saw that something was wrong as soon as he appeared in the morning, and I felt that we should get it hot, though I did not know how.

The old doctor had all the English prisoners sent for, and incredible as it may seem, every wound that was healed was deliberately reopened and plugged, while wounds that were not healed were probed inside and all the newly-formed flesh was destroyed. Many of us suffered terribly for a long time as the result of the visit to us of the old man who had lost his son in fair fight.

My wound was finally healed on July 25th, exactly nine months from the day on which my arm was taken off.

My sole object now was to get away from the horrible country and the more horrible people, and, thank God, I managed to do it. The refusal to exchange me was a bitter blow, but I soon pulled up and set to work to get away. Accordingly, when I reached Wesel, I reported myself as a private, and I was reckoned as a private and put in the list for exchange. I was sent to Aix-la-Chapelle.

Soon after this I came away with other prisoners of war, and one of the most glorious moments of my life was when I set eyes again on Old England.

There is one strange incident that I have kept to the last.

I have said that when I was shot on outpost I was stripped. My jacket must have been thrown aside, for next day a chum of mine picked it up and put it in his pack, thinking I had been killed, and meaning to bring it home, if he lived, as a relic. During many a long day and hard fight he carried that extra burden in his pack—no little thing to do—then he himself was wounded and sent home. He brought my jacket with him, and now I have it, and shall always treasure it as a memento of my war-days. The jacket is smothered in blood.

There are about 28,000 Britishers still in Germany, suffering as I suffered—some worse. They want releasing. The only way to release them is to end the war, and the only way to end the war is the cooperation of every man and woman, old and young, rich and poor, working for one object—Victory.

CHAPTER III

GASSED NEAR HILL 60

[When the Germans plunged the civilised world into this appalling war, one of their big hopes was that the sons of the Motherland would desert her in the hour of her greatest need. Never was a greater miscalculation made, even in a war which has become notorious for enemy miscalculations, for her Colonies rallied round Great Britain in a manner that has covered them with lasting glory. A particularly splendid contingent hurried over from Canada to our shores, and went into the most severe training, lasting through an uncommonly bad winter. In due course it left England, and entered almost at once into some of the hardest and most deadly fighting of the whole campaign—the conflict at the village of St. Julien, in the region of the famous Hill 60, where many troops fell gloriously in repelling the attempts of the Germans to hack their way through to Calais. In their determination to succeed, the Germans deliberately adopted the devilish device of poison-gas. How even that cowardly expedient failed is told in this story by Lance-Corporal R. G. Simmins, of the 8th Battalion Canadian Infantry, 90th Winnipeg Rifles.]

When I recall my experiences at the front, I am particularly struck by the circumstance that the thing which stands out most clearly in my mind is not the actual campaigning, not the long and weary times in the trenches, not even artillery, rifle, or bayonet work, but the coming of the poison-gas. I myself was gassed in the furious fighting at St. Julien.

I will get right at things quickly. Towards the end of April the Canadian Division was holding a line near Ypres, which was not far short of three miles in extent. That line ran north-west from Poelcapelle-Paschendaile Road, and at the end joined up with the French. Three infantry brigades with artillery comprised the division, the first being in reserve, the second on the right of the third, and the third connecting with the French.

We were in the salient of Ypres which was known to be weak, but the holding of which was of vast importance. I am proud to think that I am one of the Canadian Contingent to whom the big task of keeping back the German hosts at that point was given, and that I fought with men who gave their lives in stopping the German attempt to hack a way through to Calais, so as to have a very near blow at England. Placed as we were placed, it was possible to see the battle being fought on three sides, and this was uncommonly interesting.

We were, of course, in trenches, quite near the Germans, but between us there ran a ridge which is known as a hogback, so that there was a somewhat formidable natural barrier between the opposing forces. We were so near to the famous Hill 60 that we heard the explosion there and the subsequent battle when we were in billets at Ypres. The hill had been mined with six or seven tons of dynamite, the explosion of which was enough to change even the appearance of the hill.

There was a fine smart affair on the night of April 17th, when about a mile of German trenches was taken, and I saw about 2000 German prisoners being escorted away. Their uniforms were shabby, and their equipment was not what it ought to have been, but the men themselves appeared to be remarkably fit and well cared for.

We had gone into the trenches after marching through Ypres, where the chimney-pots were tumbling about our ears, and we were expecting very hot times; but the hogback prevented us from seeing the Germans, and of course kept us out of their sight. But there were German snipers everywhere, and they took good care to harass us.

I had charge of a section of bomb-throwers, and we did our best to hurl these strange but quite legitimate weapons at the enemy. At first the bombs were homely contrivances, made of jam-tins filled with explosives; but later they were made under War Office control, and were far superior to the primitive articles which we manufactured ourselves.

In such a war and in such a place it is not easy to tell of what was done by individuals, because so many splendid acts are unobserved; but I call to mind the coolness and resource of my own platoon officer, Lieutenant McLeod. He was dashing all over the place, encouraging his men at every point, and doing things all round in fine style. I was talking to him quite a lot in the thick of things, and was specially struck by his calmness and the wonderful effect his example had upon the men.

One outstanding performance of his was to run, in broad daylight, from battalion headquarters to the trenches—a pretty brave achievement, when you bear in mind that a running man presents an almost certain target to snipers.

In this connection, I call to mind the case of a section commander who was in a trench. He wished that a certain thing should be done, and by way of indicating his desire he held up his hand, with palm extended. That must have been a small enough target, in all conscience, but it was no sooner in the air than it was pierced by five German bullets. If a hand can be so effectively fired at, what chance to escape has the body of a man?

This trench warfare was uncommonly exhausting. You never knew what was going to happen, or what you would be called upon to do; but it was astonishing to find how soon you could adapt yourself to circumstances.

I recall an occasion when we had been forced to retire at one point and get into a communication trench; we were taken aback by the discovery that it was not deep enough. We had to dig ourselves in. That was not a hard matter for the boys who had their entrenching-tools, but I had lost mine, and the only thing left to do was to try rabbit tactics. So I began to dig myself in with my fingers, and I have a distinct recollection of tearing and scooping at the ground like an animal scuttling for shelter. Luckily the ground was soft and yielding, or I should not have had a chance with such poor tools. As it was, my fingers were torn and bleeding long before the digging-in process was completed.

I have given you a general understanding of the task that fell to the Canadian Contingent to accomplish; but as I have said, it is not the actual fighting that dwells in one's memory.

We soon settled down to the ordinary ways of war, and took them as a matter of course. While in training in England we had heard and read a good deal about the fighting, and had become accustomed to it; while as for any such discomforts as heavy rain and sodden ground, they did not trouble us. Not even Flanders could give us worse trials of this sort than we had known while wintering on Salisbury Plain.

The boys took the fighting and the hardships as part of the day's work, and there was neither grumbling nor protesting; but that state of things was changed like magic when there was sprung upon us the most cowardly, dastardly, and dirty means of fighting that the world has ever known. This was the use of poison-gas by the Germans—a device which instantly put them out of consideration as civilised combatants, and stamped them for ever as dishonourable soldiers of a dishonoured country.

This poison-gas came upon us unseen, insidiously, and without the slightest warning in the one case; and in the other it rolled down upon us literally as a cloud.

It is hard to speak calmly of this unprecedented form of

warfare, but I will try to tell exactly what happened, and I think I can do that, because when I was a medical student I particularly interested myself in chemistry.

It was on Saturday, the 24th, that our Brigade had their first experience of gas. We had been shelling the German trenches all day, and were standing to, expecting an attack by the enemy. We naturally looked for the employment of the usual methods, and were ready to receive the Germans when they showed themselves. We were strongly entrenched, and many a keen eye was kept on the hostile ground, watching for the appearance of the enemy. But not a sight of a German was to be had; there was no commotion, no excitement, no appearance of anything uncanny or uncommon, yet there was coming towards us a German weapon which was neither honest artillery nor small arms—poison-gas.

There was nothing to be seen in the air, yet suddenly, and without any apparent cause, we were overpowered by a smell exactly like nasturtium, but infinitely stronger and more pungent. The similarity noticed is remarkable, for doesn't nasturtium come from Latin words which really mean a nose-twister? Anyway, there we were in our trenches, unexpectedly overpowered by a horrible acrid smell and an invisible gas.

A lot of the boys—fine, splendid, honest fellows, who did not understand the meaning of any kind of warfare that is not honourable and aboveboard, were utterly unable to fathom the mystery, and they seemed to think that it was the kind of pest that had to be taken with the other discomforts of campaigning in the Low Country.

"What the deuce is it?" they asked.

It was not until the whole unspeakable visitation was over that most of the men realised what had happened, and that the Germans had tried to blind us as a preliminary to annihilation. Like so many more of the German hopes, this did not develop on the lines that had been planned.

This was the first poison-gas attack that we experienced, and I am thankful to say that on the whole it was a failure; but when you remember that we were utterly unready for such a filthy form of fighting, and that we had no means of combating it or nullifying its effects, you will realise the extreme disadvantage of the contest from the point of view of the Canadians.

I have said that it was about four o'clock in the afternoon when we had our first experience of the poison-gas. Now that I am talking of the thing it strikes me as a strange coincidence that it was at about four o'clock in the morning when we had our second visitation.

We had got into our stride and settled down to hard hammering and what you might call routine campaigning. Then came the morning of Saturday, April 24th, when the sun rose ten minutes before five o'clock, which means that at about four o'clock day was breaking.

Most of us were asleep; but in war time there is no such thing as universal rest for men, and our sentries were posted and keeping watchful eyes upon the German lines. It is said that the darkest hour comes just before the dawn, and I think there is no doubt that man's lowest vitality is reached at that particular period. At any rate, the Germans probably thought so, for they planned a specially fatal attack upon us in the grey hours of this April morning.

While looking round in the cheerless dawn one or two of our sentries saw a yellowish kind of cloud coming towards us, over the hogback, and travelling pretty fast. The sight was unusual enough to be noticed, but no one who saw it had the slightest idea what it really was, until we were enveloped in the filthy folds; then we knew that it was poison-gas.

The cloud rolled on, and as it got quite close to us I noticed that it was about eight feet or twelve feet high, a deep, dense yellow at the bottom, and becoming lighter towards the top, so diffuse, indeed, that it was almost indistinguishable from the atmosphere. It is not easy exactly to convey an understanding of what the cloud really was, because few men have ever seen anything like it; but it might well be described as a moving mass of yellow, fat filth, insufferably loathsome. The poison-gas, the chief constituent of which I took to be chlorine, was about twice as heavy as air, and, consequently, it travelled along the surface of the ground.

I saw the yellow cloud come, I watched it as it enveloped us, and I observed it as it rolled away behind us and went towards Ypres, gradually losing force as it was absorbed in the air. In addition to being so favourably situated, we had just had a rum ration—and plenty of it. I do not know whether the spirit did us any good, but it certainly did not do us the least harm, and may have helped to nullify the effects of the poison-gas.

Our salient, vulnerable and undoubtedly attractive to the Germans, was rushed by them, and they succeeded in breaking through and occupying a trench about a hundred yards away from our own and parallel with it. They came on with wonderful steadiness, advancing just as if they were on parade, scarcely breaking step at all. They came out of their trenches about a dozen at a time, formed two long lines, and literally seemed to walk over into the trench, though we were peppering at them all the time.

25

They kept up an excellent covering fire, with the result that a good many of our own men were shot.

This was fair, open fighting, the sort of thing that a soldier expects, and into the spirit of which he can enter. It gave opportunities, too, for the display of the best qualities of warfare, and these were shown by a man I knew very well, Company Sergeant-Major F. W. Hall, of my company. In spite of a very heavy and at that time fatal fire, the sergeant-major rushed out from the shelter of his trench to bring in a wounded man who was lying in the open. He seemed to bear a charmed life, for he got clear of the trench and was untouched by the fire of the enemy.

The sergeant-major managed, by good fortune which seemed miraculous, to get as far as the wounded man; he seized him and started with his burden for safety. In fact he actually got him as far as the trench, then, when the worst seemed over and security was just within his reach, when he was getting over the parapet and men were loudly cheering him because of his success, he was shot and killed. But the uncommon courage of the action had been noticed, and later on, to the real gratification of all the Canadians, and especially those who knew him, the announcement was made that the dead hero had been awarded the Victoria Cross. Hall's men were terribly shattered by the enemy's rifle and machine-gun fire; but in spite of it all they held their ground, and the living remnant won great glory.

It was not long before I dropped. I did not recover till the fight had swept away to my right. Then I reported to an artillery officer who was near, and he showed me the way to Ypres, telling me also to go into the city for hospital treatment.

I cannot close my yarn without mention of Captain Northwood's Company—No. 4. The company was not relieved—it could not be, because of the heavy call on troops—but it fought on doggedly till two platoons were captured. Yet there were no prisoners made except at a bitter cost to the Germans.

There were many heroes that day in No. 4 Company. I cannot name them all, but I must mention two of them who stand out pre-eminent—"Box-car" Kelly (now a King's Corporal), and Corporal Sandford. Kelly did everything in his power to rally some of the British troops who were near him, while Sandford, a section-commander, did as much by his example of splendid courage as any officer I know.

That is my story.

If space permitted I might tell of Corporal Degan and his gallant band of hand-grenaders; how they bravely fought when hemmed in by the enemy; of Lieutenant Owens, who stood with an automatic pistol in each hand, cheering and swearing in the same breath, defending his comrades and destroying the Germans; of Sergeant Nobel (now a captain), who repaired a telephone-wire under an annihilating cannonade from German guns, and a score of other splendid fellows who utterly forgot themselves and their extremity, and risked their all upon the hazard of the glorious common cause.

CHAPTER IV

A LINESMAN IN GALLIPOLI

*[A vivid understanding of the work which our
soldiers did in Gallipoli during the earlier stages of the
operations in the Dardanelles, and of the strange
happenings which were of daily occurrence in fighting the
German-led Turks, is given by this story, which is told by
Private John Frank Gray, 5th Battalion Wiltshire
Regiment.]*

Everybody knows how the transport River Clyde, with two
thousand British soldiers packed in her, was deliberately run ashore
on V Beach, at the southern point of the Gallipoli Peninsula. Great
holes had been cut in her steel sides, to make doors through which
the men could get ashore when she was hard and fast, without
embarking in any sort of craft. Land they did, in the end, though
they suffered heavily through the Turks' terrific fire. I did not see
that famous and wonderful performance, but I disembarked, with
my regiment, close to the transport while she was still aground. We
had almost the same experience as the troops from the River Clyde
had gone through. We forced a landing, in spite of barbed wire
entanglements in the water, traps which had caught many a fine
fellow and held him till the enemy's fire got him. It is odd to talk of
wire entanglements in the sea, grabbing and tearing you as you
plunge into the water, to wade ashore; but there they were, one
more new feature in a war that has been full of strange and devilish
things. Before we landed in Gallipoli we had experience of
transport, trawler, barge and pinnace; and we were no sooner at the
end of the voyage from England than we were under deadly fire and
in the thick of it.

We went right into the firing-line, and the Turks gave us more
than a warm reception—it was hot. We were under fire all the time
we were landing, but we had the uncommon good luck to suffer no
loss. As we forced our way ashore we saw plenty of evidence of the
desperate nature of the adventure of the men of the River Clyde; but
we were too much absorbed in our own affairs to pay much heed to
what had happened to other fellows.

We had got ashore on July 16th at Seddul Bahr, and stayed
there all night. So that we should be as comfortable as possible we

made dug-outs in the face of the cliff. The cliff at that place is very hard, and we had plenty of blasting to do, as well as work with pick and shovel.

My mates and I had put plenty of elbow-grease into our own particular job, and had finished our dug-out and got into it, to be cosy for the night. It was very much like animals going to bed. We were worn out, and lost no time in going to sleep. I had gone off soundly and knew nothing till I was roughly roused by some fellows shouting, "Wake up! Wake up! Three of our chaps are buried alive!"

We did not need a second rousing. We all sprang up and rushed to a spot not far away, where we saw that there had been a fall of earth and rock, and we dug harder than we had ever dug before. At the end of it, having dug to a depth of three feet, and thrown the earth and rock away from us, we came across three poor chaps of my company who had been buried by a fall of earth, caused by them digging too far into the ground to give them shelter. They had undermined too much, and the earth-roof had collapsed and crushed them. We saw at once that there was no hope—the men looked as if they had been killed on the spot: they must have been dead an hour—but we put them on stretchers and the field ambulance men did all they could. But it was too late. Next day we dug graves for them and put crosses over. There are some fine graveyards out there, well cared for, and with barbed wire fences to preserve them. While we were burying our comrades the Turks fired on us continuously, and this had to serve as the last volleys over the fallen. That solemn and tragic beginning of my experiences after landing at Gallipoli will never fade from my mind.

Even at this early stage I noticed the extraordinary luck of war. Some of the King's Own Lancasters had been in the trenches for fourteen days, and during the whole of that time they had had only twenty casualties. They left the trenches and came right up alongside of us, on a little bit of a mound. The Turks must have got wind that a lot of troops were on the move, for the shrapnel came bursting over the lot of us, especially the Lancasters, who in less than half an hour lost more than forty men, fourteen being killed and the rest wounded. Four or five of our own fellows were hit, so that we escaped lightly, and were able to send our stretcher-bearers to give a hand in getting the wounded soldiers to hospital.

The burying alive of men and the loss of men who had spent a fortnight in the trenches unscathed, were the things I saw when I was spending my first night in Gallipoli, so I can very fairly say that we landed right in the thick of it. It was a hot start, and it did not get cooler, for on the following morning, when we were on the way to the trenches at Achi Baba, we were under constant shrapnel fire. We crawled and crept up as best we could, using roads, or rather tracks, which had been made by the 29th Division. It was fearfully hot, we were heavily laden, and there was nothing but prickly scrub and rock and stifling dust about, and bursting shell all the time. But we forged slowly ahead, making the best of it, and thankful when we got into one of the little ravines which abound there, and make first-rate natural trenches—thankful because we got shelter without having to dig for it. In this advance some of our chaps fell, and the ravines formed their resting-places. The graves were filled in and crosses put over to tell how the soldiers had died. I might say here that whenever it was possible to do so, an Army chaplain read the Burial Service; but often enough a funeral had to take place with no chaplain near at hand.

An advance like this is a slow business. You go in single file, keeping your heads well down, because of the stray bullets from snipers. The Turkish snipers are dead shots—I will tell you more about them later. At the end of our dodging and ducking and crawling in single file we got into a support trench, and I began to breathe a bit more freely, because I thought that here at any rate I was safe. But we had no sooner reached the front-line trenches than the Turks started shelling us, and very quickly I thought that the very end of me had come. There was a tremendous crash just overhead, then a horrible rumbling, then I was knocked down in a heap, and all I knew was that a shell had burst in the trench and that I was buried in a mass of earth and rock. I was bruised and stunned—so were four of my chums who were near me; but we had had better luck than the three poor fellows who had been buried by the fall of earth above them, and pretty soon we had worried our way out of the heap of muck and were staring at each other—and I shall never forget that incident, if it is only because of the stupid way in which we stared at each other, and never said a word. We were making tea when the shell burst, and were looking forward to a cosy meal; but here we were, staring at each other in surprise, wondering what the dickens the matter was, till we looked around and saw what sorry objects we were, and that the tea gear had been scattered all over the place. When we had got over our fright—and what's the use of saying that we weren't scared?—we saw the grim humour of it, and laughed and pulled ourselves together, thankful that we were still in the land of the living.

That was part of our early introduction to shell fire, and we very soon learned that you never know what sort of a trick a shell is up to. Shells are very deceiving. You hear their peculiar and horrible whistle and think that they are going to burst anywhere except where they do.

30

When we had pulled ourselves together we left our shattered trench and went into another part of the trench, to pull round a bit and get out of the shrapnel bombardment. But within three hours we were back again and settled down, wondering what the coming night had in store for us. We were in for another surprise, though at that time, of course, we did not know it.

This surprise took the shape of an attack upon us by hand-grenades, or bombs. It was pitch dark; but the blackness was lit up near us in patches, caused by the explosion of the bombs. We got half a dozen of them, and as it was clear that some Turks had crept towards us from their firing-line, which was only about 200 yards away, we sent out a sergeant and five or six men to hunt the bomb-throwers. You might as well have looked for a needle in a haystack as try to find Turks who were hiding in the darkness in the shrubs or the ravines; at any rate, our chaps did not see or hear anything of the Turks, and they had to come back without doing anything. There was no doubt that the Turks had crept up to us quite close and then hurled their bombs; but we were lucky to escape with only one man slightly wounded, though if the bombers had had any luck we should have been blown to pieces. These intensely dark nights were always very trying because of these attacks. It was an immense relief when the moonlight nights came, because then the Turks dared not try their tricks on. There was always the guard, of course, two hours on and two hours off. This gave a great sense of protection; but the guard work itself gave you the creeps. You were on the rack all the time, fancying that you saw some one approaching when as a matter of fact there was no one near. There was always the chance, too, of being picked off by a sniper who used horrible explosive bullets. One of our men was struck down, and when we went up to him and removed his helmet we saw at once that an explosive bullet had been used, for the skull was completely shattered. You could always tell when these awful things had been used, from the appearance of the sandbags. The bullets would strike and explode, and smash the sandbags so badly that it took us all our time to make the damage good. You dare not put even a periscope above the trench; if you did a sniper got a bullet through it before you knew where you were.

It was all tremendously exciting, and there was never a chance of being dull or downhearted. The system of trenches was amazing, turning and twisting everywhere in the most wonderful manner. We made the most of these complications, too, by naming the trenches Oxford Street, Regent Street, and so on, with Clapham Junction and the like for important junctions of trenches. These names, which were chalked up or put on boards, were most useful in helping you to find your way about, and sometimes very amusing misunderstandings arose.

"Do you know where Oxford Circus is?" a chap asked me one day.

"Rather!" I told him, proud to throw light on his ignorance, and I began to tell him, till he cut me short by snapping that he wasn't talking about London, but the trenches. We got many a good laugh out of these little misunderstandings; for out at the front you are always ready to make the most of the smallest joke. You needed all the cheerfulness you could get, too, because of the awful sights that constantly met you and the endless peril you were in. I shall never forget one of the very first things my eyes saw in those opening days of my campaigning in Gallipoli. We got to the spot at Achi Baba where the Munsters and the Dublin Fusiliers, during a gallant advance, had been enfiladed by machine-gun fire and literally mown down. From the trench we had occupied we could see the men lying just as they had fallen, while trying to take cover. There they were, on the open ground, absolutely riddled with bullets, and with their packs on, and their rifles and bayonets and everything else. They had been lying there for about a fortnight, because it was impossible to do anything in the way of burying them, owing to the enemy's incessant fire and sniping.

Things hereabouts were particularly horrible. We went into a Turkish trench that had been taken, and started to make a fire-trench. We pulled away the old sandbags and dug away at the parapet with our picks. There was a horrible stench, but we were used to smells and did not take much notice of it till we found that the picks had a lot of foul stuff on them which we could not account for; but we soon discovered that the parapet was composed of the dead bodies of Turks which had been piled up and just covered with earth, the sandbags being placed on the top of the wall of corpses.

In this same trench there was a well which had been covered with planks. Naturally enough we began to explore it, not that we expected to get anything to drink from it, and when we had removed the planks we found that the well, which we calculated was ten or twelve feet deep, had a lot of dead Turks in it. We counted six of them, and had enough of the job, so we put the planks back, and felt that our curiosity had been satisfied.

When we had been there four or five days and were getting used to the appearance of the country, we saw a Turk just peeping over the top of a little mound, with his rifle pointing towards us and in the attitude of firing. We felt sure that we had caught a sniper, and two or three shots were promptly fired. The Turk was still there, and it was clear that he had been shot. Later on we were able to get near him, and then we saw that he was black with flies and had been shot through the eye while sniping; but not shot by us, because when we shook him his head fell off, showing that he had been dead for some time. We saw another Turk who was sitting against a tree. We went up and found that he, too, was dead. He looked a mere skeleton; but he was swathed in clothing and equipment in the most extraordinary fashion. His trousers were all rags, and his tunic was all patches of differently coloured cloths; he had three shirts and two belts on, and we wondered how he had stuck so many clothes in such stifling weather.

I had an exciting adventure one day—a bit too exciting to be altogether pleasant. I and another chap had been sent out to an artillery position which was called Clapham Junction Station, to get some corrugated iron. We had a long way—two and a half miles—to go, and it was necessary to keep to the cover of the trenches whenever we could do so. We were able to do that for most of the way, going through the very trenches which had been dug by the poor chaps of the Munsters and Dublin Fusiliers who had fallen. We got to the end of our journey, quite near the French lines, and then started back with our corrugated iron. Burdened in this way, we found that one of the trenches was too narrow for us to get along, and we were forced to make our way across open country for about 500 yards. As soon as we left the shelter of the trench the sun shone on our galvanised metal and gave the Turks a good target. We promptly had three or four shells bursting near us, and we lost no time in doubling over the open ground, staggering along with the iron sheets, and thankful when we were under shelter again, with a farewell shell or two to show us what a narrow squeak we had had. I picked up one of these shells, which had not burst, and kept it a long time, meaning to bring it home as a souvenir, but I found it a nuisance and had to throw it away.

We were constantly seeing strange sights and learning how cunning the Turks were. One morning I saw some Australians bring in a Turk who was wearing one of our uniforms. The tunics had white patches on them, so that our artillery could distinguish us, and it was one of these that the fellow wore. He had no doubt taken it from a dead British soldier, and so dressed, he had joined a party of Australians who were drawing water at a well. He kept his mouth shut, and might have gone undiscovered, but he and an Australian began quarrelling, then fighting, and that gave him away, because he could not speak English. They shot him, as a spy, the following morning.

At the same place—I am now speaking of W Beach, where we were resting—we saw a Turkish sniper on the top of a hill. We sent out two or three times to try and get him, but failed; but at last he was caught while robbing one of our fellows who was dead. The sniper had shot him, and now he was out for plunder. When we had this sniper in hand we found that we had got hold of a very dangerous customer, a man who had done a lot of mischief amongst our fellows. He had gone about his sniping in a very business-like way, and had established himself in a spot which commanded points which had to be continually passed by our stretcher-bearers and working parties. A good many of the R.A.M.C. chaps were hit, and it was curious that most of the wounds were about the knee. We discovered that these wounds were the result of the sniper's low firing—he was very near the ground and had pretty nearly complete control of this particular spot. Our fellows used to double round it for all they were worth, but they were not fast enough to dodge the Turk's bullets. When we examined his dug-out we found three rifles fixed on tripods, which were always trained on the spots where our fellows had to pass. In addition to that he had a machine-gun, and this he used for firing on our men when he knew that it was meal-time and that they were in clusters. It was a great relief when his account was settled.

Aircraft fighting has developed enormously during the war, and I saw an exciting fight between three of our aeroplanes and two of the Turks. We had got a bit used to aeroplanes, for a Taube had swooped over us and dropped a chance bomb which blew up the quartermaster's stores. Three bombs fell about a hundred yards away, and I noticed that the noise they made when they came through the air was just like the whistle of a railway engine. In the fight I am talking about our fellows brought down one of the Turkish machines, and they made a hard chase after the other, but it got away. It was a really thrilling fight, and our chaps got tremendously excited over it. We had been warned of an attack from the air by three blasts on a whistle, and that was the signal to take shelter and to cover up the guns with tarpaulins, to hide them. During these attacks you are supposed never to look up, but the fight was so splendid and our chaps got so excited that the warning was forgotten in many cases, and chaps were peeping over the parapets and some were actually standing up on the parapets. Poor fellows! Turkish snipers spotted them and got three with their bullets. I was only about a hundred yards away when they were killed. Their loss, which was a lesson to all of us, cast quite a gloom over our victory in the air.

After being in the trenches at Achi Baba for sixteen days we went back to Lemnos, a big naval base about four and a half hours' distant by transport. We were supposed to have a week's rest, but

34

we were at Lemnos only three days. At the end of that time we went back to the Peninsula and landed at Anzac, and went straight up to the firing-line, which had been made at Chunuk Bahr—and our regiment got absolutely cut up. It was one of the things that will happen in a war like this.

We had gone up into the trenches and nothing much happened while we were there. After our spell in the trenches we were taken up into a gulley for twenty-four hours' rest and sleep. We were in high spirits at the prospect of such a change, and we took our equipment off and made a few dug-outs and got into them and settled down, and very comfortable and contented we were. But our rest and peace were smashed at dawn on the following morning, when we were thrown into confusion by a heavy Turkish attack. The Turks had advanced into the firing-line on the opposite side of the hill. There were plenty of them and they had machine-guns, while we were quite helpless, having no rifles nor equipment—indeed, many of us had not even our jackets on, as we were taking it easy.

There was quite a stampede for the time being, and some one passed the order, "Every man for himself!" It was a mistake, I am certain, but it added immensely to the confusion. That awful alarm caused some of our unarmed chaps to make a bolt for it, the result of temporary panic; and now came one of those splendid bits of work which are the pride of every regiment, and which no one can do better than British soldiers.

The adjutant, Captain Belcher, rallied about seventy of the men. He pulled them together, put heart of grace into them, and shouted to them to get their rifles and bayonets and follow him. There is nothing like an heroic example at such a time. The little band rallied round the adjutant, and with wild cheers and a gallant rush they hurled themselves upon the Turks, and such was the suddenness and fury of their attack that the Turks bolted like children—and big hefty chaps they were—with our fellows, some of them almost as small as dwarfs, tearing after them with the bayonet. In this furious affair one of our men got wounded and could not walk. The adjutant picked him up and began to carry him away. As he did so the Turks opened fire on him with a machine-gun, and he must have been riddled—I never saw anything more of him. At the same time Lieutenant Ratcliffe, who had been wounded, was being carried off on a stretcher. He seemed to think that the chance of escape was hopeless, and so he said to his bearers, "Put me down and look after yourselves, boys. I shall be all right." It was a hard thing to do, but the men obeyed, and all of us who could do so got away from that fatal spot, which we were far too weak to hold, in spite of the success of the adjutant's rally, and at last we got back to the beach.

It was then that we compared notes and heard of what had happened in various places, and the roll having been called we supposed that every man who could escape had reached the beach. But two nights afterwards we formed a search party, and went back up the hill and were lucky enough to find and bring back with us about a dozen poor fellows who had been lying all that time on the battlefield. From this rescue we supposed that there must be other men alive at the top of the hill; but there was no chance of reaching them in the daytime, and we could not go at night, for the searchlights from our own warships swept the hillside and lit it up so brilliantly that any search party would have been shown up to the snipers. So we did no more, and soon we were forgetting; for we were hard at work on fatigue, helping the Engineers to build a new firing-line, a trench about 1400 yards long. Then happened a thing so strange that it seemed beyond belief, like men rising from the dead. Fifteen days had passed since the fight, and no one dreamed that there could possibly be survivors, yet there appeared at the beach headquarters two terribly worn and haggard men, Lance-Corporal A. G. Scott of my company, and Private R. Humphries, another of our chaps. We were amazed to see them, and far more amazed to hear their story, which was that they and Private W. J. Head had been up in the hill for fifteen days and nights, unable to get away, and living on the biscuits and water that they had taken from the haversacks and bottles of dead men. The Turks, they said, used to pass them and shake hands with them, but would never give them any food or water. The three used to grope about in the daytime to get food and drink, and the Turks sniped at them whenever they got the chance. Head was quite unable to escape, having had two bad wounds. Scott and Humphries, desperate at last, crawled away and managed to reach our regimental headquarters and tell their wonderful story, and it was no sooner heard than a search party was organised, and, with Scott and Humphries as guides, went back to the old fighting-place—a slow and dangerous job. On the first night they found nothing, but on the next night the relieving party came across three fellows and brought them down. Head was amongst them—he had been out getting more biscuits and water, and while doing so his right arm was smashed by a machine-gun which was trained on him. The body of the poor lieutenant was found, with several bayonet wounds, and he, like all the other officers who fell, had been completely stripped by plunderers. The bodies had not a thing on them.

The survivors of those awful days and nights on the hillside—

from August 10th to August 26th—had such a welcome as can be given only to those who return when they have been given up as lost, and Scott and Head and Humphries have been awarded the Distinguished Conduct Medal. There have been some extraordinary incidents in this war, but not many are stranger than this adventure of this little band of men for what must have seemed an endless fortnight, and none that will stand out more finely in the annals of the Wiltshires.

There was so much to be seen and done in the three months I spent in the Near East that it is not easy to describe everything, and I must now mention only one or two things more. Very clearly in my mind stands out our attack on Chocolate Hill, after the warships had bombarded it for three days. We watched the naval guns at work, and saw the terrible havoc they caused—many a Turk we saw flying up in the air when the shells burst. When we advanced over Salt Lake we had to cross a hayfield, under a very heavy fire. The bursting shrapnel knocked many a fellow down, and we could not stop to help them or pick them up—and that was terribly hard on us, for the hayfield had taken fire and it meant that a lot of helpless men were burned alive. I saw one poor chap, a Yeoman, struck by shrapnel. This made him completely helpless for the time, and the fire got at him and burnt half his left leg off; but I am thankful to say that he managed, by a truly desperate effort, to crawl away, and he got out of it at the finish. We were in the advance, and as the field was catching fire just as we got out of it, we escaped the worst, which was to be caught in the middle, so that even those who were fit and could make a rush were badly burned and suffering intensely before they could get clear of the horrible ring of fire.

I can tell you of an extraordinary incident that happened in the Chocolate Hill attack to a man of the South Wales Borderers. In the second bayonet charge he drove his steel into a Turk—and it broke. Off he dashed without his bayonet, and rushed with his chums to the next trench, where he plumped into a Turk who was crawling through a hole. Knowing that his broken bayonet was useless, he clubbed his rifle and let the Turk have the butt. The blow smashed the butt clean off, and the Borderer tumbled down. The Turk, who was not much hurt, sprang back from his hole, and jumped to his feet with the Englishman fairly at his mercy. Luckily for the Borderer a pal rushed up and saved him by settling the Turk. It was an extraordinary thing that the Borderer first broke his bayonet and then bashed his butt, which came off as clean as a whistle.

Another thing that happened was this: An officer was wounded and fell. One of the men of his regiment heard the report that the officer was missing. "I'll go and find him," he said, and off he went. After an hour's search he found the officer and asked him if he could walk. "No," the officer told him, so the man picked him up and started to carry him—a hard and dangerous job. While the officer was being carried he was wounded again, a bullet striking him. "Put me down," he ordered, "and look after yourself." "No, sir," said the man; "if you're game, I am." And game he was, too, for he got him safely away, and the officer, to show his gratitude, made the man a present of his revolver and a silver flask. When the soldier rejoined his regiment they took the revolver away; but he kept the flask as a memento, carefully wrapped up in all sorts of things, very proud of the gift from the officer, who had said, "I shall never forget you!" The officer was mortally wounded, and died before they could get him into the hospital ship.

It was round Chocolate Hill that we made our queerest find of all—women snipers. There was a kind of blockhouse which had been a farmhouse, and it had a very fine well, which had some very fine water—a precious thing. There was a big run on the well, and a lot of fellows were shot by snipers who could not be traced, till a fellow in a Welsh regiment swore that he could see some one moving in some trees not very far away. A machine-gun was brought up, and fifty rounds or so were fired into the trees, which dropped some very rare fruit—four men Turks and one woman Turk, all snipers. When we went up we found that they were almost naked, and had their faces and hands and bodies and rifles painted green to match the trees. And there they roosted, like evil birds, potting at our chaps whenever they got the chance, which was pretty often. This was such a good haul that firing was directed on all the trees, and more snipers were brought down, including several women. Some of the women wore trousers, like the men, and some had a kind of full grey-coloured skirt. They were as thin as rats, and looked as if they had had nothing to eat for months. I think there were six or seven women snipers caught in the trees, and it is said that the Turks have women in the trenches; but I don't know if that is true. I saw one woman sniper who had been caught by the New Zealanders. I don't know what was done with her; but as the men came back they told us they had bagged her in a dug-out, where she had a machine-gun and a rifle, and that she seemed to have been doing a very good business in sniping.

Dysentery knocked me out in the end, and after spending a fortnight in hospital at Malta I had "H.S.B."—hospital-ship berth— put opposite to my name. I came home in a hospital ship, a foreigner, which made me thankful when I landed at Southampton and entered a good old English hospital train bound for Manchester.

CHAPTER V

AN ANZAC'S ADVENTURES

["When the German blood-stained Eagle and its vulture-hearted Chief
Made war on little Belgium, they held the fond belief
The British Lion had grown too tame and dared not interfere;
But when old England called the roll, Australia answered, 'Here!'"

That is part of one of the marching songs of the Anzacs, and it will go down to history as surely as "John Brown's Body" has descended to our own generation. It was written for a particular Australian battalion, but it applies to all the glorious regiments that have won immortality in Gallipoli. This Anzac's story shows how the sons of the Empire rallied to the call of the Motherland, and helped so much to carry out that unexampled undertaking in the Dardanelles of which our descendants alone can be the fairest judges. The narrator is Trooper Rupert Henderson, of the 6th Australian Light Horse.]

I was a sheep overseer when I joined the Australian Light Horse. Before that I was a jackaroo on a twenty-thousand acre station. What is a jackaroo? Well, a cross between a kangaroo and a wallaroo, and applied to a man, it means that he does anything that comes along. My boss's station was twenty-five miles from the nearest town; but that's nothing of a distance in Australia, and we used to have some merry parties when we had a day off, and drove or rode to the town for a change. And it was to the town that we swarmed just after the war broke out—bosses and men, rich and poor. A fine young fellow, a squatter's son, Mr. David McCulloch, wrote and asked me to join the Light Horse, and I gladly did. He tried hard to come, too, but the doctor would not pass him, and to his intense disappointment he was rejected. He came to see me twice while I was training, and both times he tried to pass; but could not get through. That was the spirit which was shown when the call came out to us to go and fight the Germans and the Turks, or anybody else that British troops were up against.

We went into camp at Rosebery Park, Sydney, which is a

racecourse. The 1st Light Horse had to sleep in the stables; but we were comfortably camped. The hard floors of the stables were very different from the comfortable beds which had been left; but the fellows were mostly horsemen from the country and didn't mind, because they were used to roughing it.

Horses, saddles, equipment and uniforms were issued to us, and we were soon doing horse and foot drill. After six weeks of this training we went to Holdsworthy, on the George's River, in the bush country. Snakes of all sorts swarm there—tiger snakes, black snakes, copperheads and deaf adders, all poisonous, as well as the carpet snakes, which are sometimes twenty feet long. They are gorgeous things, and look like bright-coloured carpets. They are non-poisonous, and our chaps let them coil round their necks and do all sorts of things. At this place there was the German internment camp, and already there were plenty of both military and civilian prisoners. The camp was not cleared—it was just barbed wire for a guard camp—but the country round it was being cleared.

We were very lucky in our training, and afterwards, too, because we were under Colonel Cox—"Fighting Charlie," we called him—who had seen service in South Africa, and was a fine soldier.

It was midsummer and harvest-time when, on December 17th, we left Holdsworthy for Sydney, and we had the remarkable experience of going through three summers in one year. We started with our own, which we left in the tropics, when we got to Egypt it was the Egyptian summer, and when we landed at the Dardanelles it was the Gallipoli summer.

In Australia, of course, everything had given place to the war, and army lorries and so on had cut the roads up frightfully. They were full of ruts and holes and deep in dust; but luckily a storm came on, and the rain made it possible for us to travel in comfort.

I shall never forget that march to the transport to embark. We marched in the night-time, but all along the route the people were waiting for us. Nobody seemed to have gone to bed, and as we marched along they cheered us and wished us luck. The people gave us drinks, and fruit, and handkerchiefs, and other souvenirs. It was a wonderful and moving sight, and the people kept it up right away to the Woolloomooloo Wharf at Sydney, where we embarked on board the White Star liner Suevic. We lay in harbour from Sunday morning till Monday afternoon. I was on guard all the time. We had plenty of visitors, some of them trying to get chaps out for a last spell ashore; but that had to be stopped, of course, and the officers sent the men down to stables. The horses of my squadron, C, were below; but the other squadrons had their horses on deck.

I am not going to dwell on the last parting and send-off. We steamed away, and on Christmas Day we were six days out and two days' sail from Albany, Western Australia. When we got there we picked up a magnificent fleet of sixteen transports and the Australian submarine AE2, which was afterwards lost. Then the war seemed to be really with us, the Anzacs, the famous word which is formed of the initials of the words "Australian and New Zealand Army Corps."

We came through Suez and Port Said, and did not go off the boats till we got to Alexandria. We stayed a night at Ismailia, and there, as the beginning of our fighting with the Turks, we came under their fire, or rather, we heard it. This made us feel that we were getting into things, and we listened with immense interest to the boom of the guns. At the same time we piled up our ship with bales of hay, as a protection, and mounted machine-guns, and fervently hoped that the Turks would come on and give us a chance against them; but we were not molested. They did not interfere with us then, but we soon had plenty to do with them.

It was March 31st when C Squadron disembarked at Alexandria and got into the train, with Major White in charge. We went to Cairo, and then unloaded our horses and took them, walking, to a place ten miles outside the city; and there, practically in the desert, we camped, and for three months we had steady mounted drill, which made us as fit as fiddles. We had real dry heat, and no rain, all the time; but this did not trouble us, being Australians, and used to droughts. But we were glad when, at the end of the three months, the order came for us to pack up our kits and leave for the Dardanelles. We had the infantry kit served out to us, and in the middle of May we were back in Cairo, where we saw a lot of our chaps who had come back wounded from the Dardanelles. We found ourselves once more at Alexandria; and then, in two days we were at the Dardanelles, of which we had heard and talked so much, and where we had been so eager to go.

We had left Egypt on a peaceful Sunday afternoon; now we were in the very thick of a wonderful and exciting war, for we were being towed ashore in pinnaces, each holding about 250 men—half the regiment—and were under heavy fire. Gunboats were booming away, shells were bursting, and aeroplanes were sweeping about the sky. All these things gave us a good idea of what was going on.

How did we take it, not being used to the business? Well, the chaps sat in the pinnaces and looked at one another, to see how they stood it. We were landing in broad daylight, the boats were packed, bullets were dropping all around us, sending nasty little spits of water up; and bullets from rifles and machine-guns were whizzing over our heads. I was watching the impression it was having on the others. Some of our chaps were wearing war medals, and I made up my mind to carry on as they were doing. If they took it all right, so would I.

They did take it all right.

As the bullets dropped round us I heard such remarks as, "By Jove! If that hit a fellow it would hurt him!" Then men would laugh.

Our colonel—I was sitting near him in the pinnace—looked stern and calm. He knew better than most of us what it meant.

We were lucky in our landing, for we had no casualties; but a lot of the other troops who were landing at the same time and in the same way were picked off. We lay off till one of the naval boats got alongside. We all tumbled into her and were taken to the beach for landing.

The Turks saw us landing and gave us five shells, but these did not hurt anybody. We were told to hurry up; but we didn't need telling to do that, and as soon as the boat was at the shore we hopped on to a little wharf and found ourselves in the thick of some Indians who were unloading sheep. So little did we need telling to hurry up, that I well remember how we rushed through the sheep in our eagerness to get to shelter.

We were in fine spirits and made the best of it; but as soon as we landed we realised what we were in for. A shell came and burst amongst a fatigue party, knocking the men about badly and wounding half a dozen, but luckily not killing anybody. This showed us how necessary it was to take cover, and when we had got some distance up the heights and were ordered to dig in, we set to work with a will, and we readily obeyed the order to keep our heads well down, as the shrapnel was bursting over the top of us.

Our regiment was keeping well together. The colonel was in a gulley just below me when a shell burst over us. It seemed to be high, and we did not realise the danger of such explosions. This shell seemed to be harmless; but I soon discovered that a fragment or bullet of it had struck the colonel in the leg. As this was the headquarters the doctor was handy, and he attended to the colonel straight away, and sent him to the beach on a stretcher. Two minutes afterwards, one of the squadron clerks got shot with a shrapnel bullet. This also happened near me, and I saw what happened to him. The bullet struck him just by the right temple—he had the closest possible shave of instant death—and carried the eye away. This chap was put out of action at once, and was sent on to Malta. About ten days later he wrote to us saying what rotten luck he had had. But he was a cheerful soul and made the best of things, though he said, very truly, "I have only had a one-eyed view of Malta!"

We got dug in. There were holes in front of us, about four feet deep, with head covering, about two feet of earth, on top of us; but these did not give much protection from shells that burst just overhead. Some of the men filled empty biscuit-tins with earth and put them alongside to protect their legs from stray and spent bullets, and these proved very useful. When we had dug in we were ordered to eat our iron-rations for tea; then, about eight o'clock, they called the regiment to fall in, as the Turks were going to attack us. We stood up as reinforcements at a place called Shrapnel Gulley—and well it deserved its name, as we soon learned, for there were a terrible lot of casualties there, especially amongst the fatigue parties which had to go to the beach for water.

You will see that we were initiated straight away. We did not know the danger of it at the time, and never thought that we should be so soon put through it after landing. But it was astonishing to see how well the chaps settled down to the business. We had been landed only a few hours, and yet we were standing to arms, waiting for the Turks to come on. We expected them with a rush, for we had been told that Enver Bey, the Minister of War, had ordered that the Anzacs were to be thrown into the sea. Well, we didn't mean to be thrown.

We were standing on open ground. There were two very high hills, and we were in the gulley at the bottom. Some of our troops were dug in on the top of the hills, and the Turks were dug in in front of us, some of them being not more than fifty yards away.

It was a pitch-dark night, and a nerve-racking job waiting for the promised onslaught. Time passed and it seemed as if the Turks would never come; but at three in the morning they let themselves loose.

The word was passed along—"The enemy is advancing in front!" and we were all ordered to stand fast till two blasts of the whistle had been sounded.

It was hard to make out anything in that inky blackness, even with the eyes of bushmen; but we knew that the Turks had crawled out of their trenches and that they were going to throw themselves upon us. Then two shrill blasts struck the still night, and instantly there was a fearful commotion, for the Turks hopped up from the ground and charged, yelling and firing, and making all sorts of deafening noises, amongst which we noticed a trumpeter doing his best to blow our own call of the "Officers' Mess." They seemed to blow anything that came along, so as to confuse us in the pitch darkness. And a startling business it was, too, to peer into the blackness and see the figures of the Turks by the light of the bursting shells and crackling rifles.

Never while I live shall I forget that fight in the first night we were ashore in Gallipoli. We did our best to see what was going on by looking through the pot-holes in the sandbags of the trenches, though at night you could look over the tops of the parapets; but it was little enough that we could make out in the darkness.

We had our magazines loaded and our bayonets fixed. The infantry alongside were in "possies," as we called them, holes dug in the trenches to keep a man from being exposed. Two men were in each "possy," one firing and the other loading for him, so that a constant fire was kept up. One of our fellows, terribly excited, had crawled up on to the sandbags, and there he stood, just seen in the darkness by the flashes of fire, for about ten minutes, when he was ordered down.

At this time I was a non-combatant, one of the stretcher-bearers, and I was just standing, waiting for somebody to get hit; so I could see everything that was going on. The shells were flying round all the time, making a fearful noise, and an Indian battery above us was doing good work. In a "possy" high above us were the machine-guns, and we could see even in the darkness what havoc they were causing amongst the enemy.

In the loud cries that arose I heard a Scotchman of our regiment shout, "Here comes a big Turk with a brick in his hand!"

We peered into the blackness and saw a big fine Turk crawling on the ground about five yards away, holding in his hand something that looked like a brick. The machine-guns got him just as he jumped up. The bullets fairly smothered him, and he dropped like a thousand of bricks. Later on I had a good look at him, and found that the thing he carried was not a brick but a bomb. He had no boots on, but his feet were wrapped in cloth, so that he made no sound. He had managed to get within ten paces of us.

The din quietened down as daylight came, which was about five o'clock. We looked eagerly around us to see what had been done, and noticed the dead Turks everywhere, many of them in clusters of half a dozen, just as they had been mown down by our machine-guns. Later on we learned that the number of the Turkish dead was 2000, so that the ground was fairly strewn with bodies.

We were ordered back to our trenches, where we had breakfast and a bit of rest; but at ten o'clock we were told to fall in again, as the Turks were making another charge. The enemy did come on, but rather half-heartedly, and they were repulsed without our aid. They had made a fine and brave dash in the night, as we saw. They never got into our trenches, but we were told that they had rushed in farther round, where the New Zealanders were; but they had been bayoneted straight away.

In the afternoon the Turks put up a white flag and asked for an armistice, to bury the dead.

A big old Turk walked towards us, and he was met by Captain R. J. A. Massie, a famous Australian amateur champion, an all-round athlete of splendid physique. The Turk was blindfolded and brought into our trenches and then taken to headquarters, and after he had been questioned an armistice was granted.

The firing ceased, and the Turks came out with all their stretcher-bearers, and our stretcher-bearers and diggers went out, too, and the burials went on—and not before they were necessary, for the stenches were awful.

This sad work was being done, when our artillery observers noticed that the Turks were bringing up guns and reinforcements from the gulley at the back of our chaps, and we were ordered to come in.

That ended the armistice for the time, and the Turks at the back were fired on and their little game stopped. Next morning there was another armistice, for it was absolutely necessary to get on with the burials. The atmosphere was almost unendurable, and, even on landing, the stench from dead mules and so on was so horrible that it nearly made me bilious.

On that second morning I was able to see that a lot of our chaps were lying between our parapet and the Turks' parapet. We made an exchange of bodies, and having got our men's identification discs, we buried them in the small trenches, so that the fighting-places became graves.

All these things that I have told about happened within thirty hours of our landing—and the fortune of war had sent some of the Anzacs to their last resting-place and put others, wounded, on the list for home. Men were sent off, their fighting careers ended, after having been in the enemy's country for only a few hours.

We were pretty philosophical over the business. I remember one of the men in my squadron saying, "If your name's on a bullet you're going to stop it." Soon afterwards a four-point-seven got him.

The Turks used to fire like mad. It was astonishing to see how many bullets they fired, but even at that early stage our men, when off duty, were asleep and taking no notice of them.

At this time we were opposite Lone Pine, attached to the 4th Australian Battalion as infantry. After the fighting we had exactly a month in the trenches, and then relieved some infantry who had had three weeks of solid fighting. We were relieved and went to a rest camp near Gaba Tepi. We had seven days there, with a good deal of excitement one way and another, and plenty of casualties, for we were being called out every day.

It was rumoured that Achi Baba was going to fall, and we were ordered into the firing-line as supports for the 5th Light Horse. The 5th were going out in front to draw the Turks' fire and keep reinforcements from going down to Achi Baba. Some of the 6th and 7th Light Horse were to stand by and act as reinforcements. My troop was in the firing-line.

The 5th hopped out right on the beach, and ran for Gaba Tepi under cover of the ridges. The 7th got up on our left. We were in the middle. A squadron of the 7th ran along under cover of the ridge, in the same direction as the 5th. They went a good while without drawing the fire of the Turks, who did not seem to notice them; but fire was opened at last.

Still the advance continued, more cautiously now, our fellows crawling when they could, for shelter. The Turks got a few lucky shells in amongst the 5th, and the casualties began to come in.

There were some odd incidents.

Our sergeant was peering through a look-out with a pair of glasses, his right hand being round them. Another sergeant said, "Let's have a peep."

Our sergeant pulled his head back and straightened himself, but still held the glasses with his hand in front of the hole.

The other sergeant was just stepping up to take the glasses, when a bullet came through the hole and went clean through the hand that still held the glasses, putting our sergeant out of action. We took him to the dressing-station, and he was not long before he was back in the firing-line, which is more than would have happened if the sergeant had been still bending down and had got the bullet in his head. He was a nice chap—a station-manager from Queensland.

In about two hours volunteers were asked for to bring in wounded Colonials from the front. There were a good many casualties by this time, and plenty for the stretcher-bearers to do.

We got to two men who, we saw at once, were very badly wounded. They were pretty well sheltered, and it was thought better to leave them where they were for the present, and not try to move them. One man had his foot blown off by shrapnel, and he was otherwise very badly wounded. A stretcher-bearer had bound him up roughly and put a tourniquet on to stop the bleeding; and another chap had carried him on his back to shelter. Several of the stretcher-bearers were killed and wounded at this time, but I do not think that the firing on them was deliberate.

The other man was a trumpeter. He was a little chap, and we called him "Scottie," because he had gone out to Australia from Scotland. He was wounded in the abdomen, and was in agony, but we managed to relieve his suffering with half a grain of morphia. The flies were swarming and were terribly troublesome. I tried to keep them off with a wet towel—I had to wet it in salt water—so that they should not annoy him. I noticed that his boots were torn, and I took them off. I then saw that his legs had not been dressed—and he had been lying there for some time. I put iodine on the wounds.

Scottie was rather cheery, and when the padre came up and said, "Well, how are you?" he answered, "I'm feeling pretty good now."

When the colonel went up to him, Scottie said, "I'm going to die!"

"Oh no, you're not," said the colonel. "You'll get all right again. Don't let that worry you. You'll soon be playing Christmas Calls for us."

To that Scottie made a reply which I shall never forget. "Yes," he said. "I shall die! I can smell ut!" That was his real expression, and I suppose he meant that he could smell death.

Scottie wanted the colonel to take charge of some little trinkets and things: his pay-book, and a photograph of two children. "Give these to the wife," he said. Then he broke into "Annie Laurie," and sang a verse of it. He sang the song fairly well. It was a good attempt for a man in the straits that he was in.

At six o'clock he died, and was buried the same night, after sundown, at the place where we were, and that was a big cutting called Chatham's Post, named after one of the officers. It was a deep cutting in the side of the hill. These two chaps were lying there on stretchers, and it was very hard for a bullet to hit them. Scottie was just taken to the back of the parade at the back of Chatham's Post, a place called Shrapnel Green. It was a green field when we first went, but it was soon trodden down and made bare by gun and rifle fire. And there Scottie was laid to rest.

From the burial we went back to the dressing-station and carried the wounded trooper—Lane, they called him—down to the beach. The padre asked Lane if he would like a "wad," that is a pannikin, of tea, and Lane said he would. I helped him to sit up, and I held the "wad" for him. He drank the tea cheerfully, though he must have been in awful agony. They took him along the beach. He did not say much, but never complained. When he did speak it was to ask, "Who's that lying there?" or "How is he getting on?" He was the best I saw the whole time I was there.

On the way to the beach there were wire entanglements, to stop the Turkish patrols. The stretcher-bearers fell into the entanglements and dropped Lane; but he never thought about himself. What he said was, "Are you hurt?" I am glad to say that he is here in England, like me, and has pretty well got over it, though he has lost his foot. Seventeen men were hit by the shell that knocked Lane out.

We settled down again to the fighting game with the Turks, who kept us very lively, especially with a gun that we called "Beachy Bill." This gun played on the beach whenever there was a sign of our movements, and it became a common thing to say, "Beachy Bill's got somebody again." That Turkish gun caused more casualties than all the rest put together. The monitors used to go for it, and I believe they bombarded it out of existence more than once. A new gun was soon at work again, but to us it was always "Beachy Bill." When we first got to Gallipoli we did not know the tricks of the trade, but everybody soon got fly, and that helped us a lot in tackling "Beachy Bill" and lessening his bag.

There's a lot more to say, but I will only tell you about one more thing, and that is the blowing up of some Turks. Our trenches and those of the Turks almost met in places, and bombs were thrown from one to the other. That was a lively exchange of greetings, but it didn't lead to much. Something more definite was wanted, and so our people began to dig a tunnel at a very narrow junction, so as to blow up the Turkish trenches, and make our own trench-line straight, instead of being, as it was, twisting and zigzag.

It was a real Turk hunt, and just the sort of work that our chaps revelled in.

This affair, like most of our scraps, was done in the darkness, which made it all the more thrilling. Well, we dug and sapped and tunnelled towards the Turks, and when everything had been got ready, powder was packed in sandbags and fuses were put to them. The deeper the sandbags the worse the explosion.

All was ready at last. The powder-bags were packed, the fuses were lit, and then the 11th and 12th Battalions began to finish the work which the artillery had begun. The guns had started at five o'clock, they went on booming till nine, then there was a fearful sound which was louder than the loudest thunder I ever heard, accompanied by an immense mass of red fire in the blackness of the night. I was two hundred yards away, but the very earth on which I stood shook and shivered with the upheaval.

As soon as the crash came our chaps hopped up and rushed the shattered trenches. They found that a big crater had been made by the explosion, and that most of the Turks had been stiffened. Those who were left were either bayoneted or bombed. The Turks did not counter-attack that day. They had had enough of it. We had a good few casualties, but it was an effort that was worth while, because it showed that if we wanted a place we could take it, and at any time we liked. I saw all this very clearly, for I was going backward and forward all the time as a stretcher-bearer.

The Turks gave us no chance and we gave them none; but at the same time they did not do anything that I would call really dirty or out of the way. A lot of them were fine fellows physically. Some of the Turkish diggers we got as prisoners had no fighting gear on them at all. They were just peasants who had been brought up to do the work.

At last I fell ill with dysentery and gastritis, and came home on a huge hospital ship, with four thousand more sick and wounded soldiers. We had a six days' run to Southampton, and had just under sixty deaths on board. They were buried at sea in batches, the biggest being eleven—and very solemn it all was.

Now I have done; but I want to tell of just one more little thing that happened here in England, where I have been in hospital, and where people have been so good to us.

It was Christmas-time, and we were having a Sunday evening service in hospital. We were asked what hymns we would like, and a chap spoke out and said, "Let's have

> 'We plough the fields and scatter
> The good seed on the land.'"

The parson was puzzled. He hardly thought we could, because it was Christmas-time and this was a harvest hymn.

"And it's harvest-time now at home in Australia," the chap said.

So we had the good old hymn, and it took us back to home twelve thousand miles away.

•••••••

I think the Anzacs did what they set out to do.

CHAPTER VI

"IMPERISHABLE GLORY" FOR THE KENSINGTONS

["By your splendid attack and dogged endurance on May 9th, you and your fallen comrades won imperishable glory for the 13th London Battalion. It was a feat of arms surpassed by no battalion in this great war." This was the fine tribute paid to the 13th (Kensington) Battalion of the London Regiment by General Sir Henry Rawlinson, commanding the 4th Army Corps, after the Kensingtons had taken part in the British advance in May between Bois Grenier and Festubert. The battalion had already greatly distinguished itself in the Neuve Chapelle operations and elsewhere. This story of some of the doings of the corps at the front is told by a member of the Kensingtons, who wishes to remain anonymous.]

The main body of the Kensingtons had gone out in October, and I left England with a draft in January, the dead of winter. We marched up to billets in Laventi, three miles from the firing-line. The place was being heavily shelled by the Germans, and amongst other buildings the church was smashed up; but the men were lucky, and I don't think that any soldiers were hit there. I shall always particularly remember that place, because it was there that I saw for the first time a man who had been killed by the enemy.

I was going along a street near an old ruined house which was being used as a soldiers' club, when I heard the noise of an exploding shell. The crash was very near, and soldiers rushed out from the ruined house to see what had happened. They told me that the shell had burst farther down the street, and that a civilian had been killed. Without any loss of time they took a door down, and using this as a stretcher they carried the dead man away, and as I watched them I realised that we were fairly in it, and I am bound to say that I was very strangely moved and deeply impressed by this little tragedy.

We realised even more fully what it all meant when for the first time at the front we put five rounds of ball ammunition in the magazines and marched off for our first spell in the trenches, between our billets and the firing-line. We started at dusk, so that we should reach the trenches just when it became dark.

There was something very solemn in going away like that towards the enemy; yet there was, of course, intense excitement and curiosity. It was not a very exhilarating start, because the country was in a very bad state, owing to the heavy January rains. There was plenty of water in the trenches when we reached them, and it was bitterly cold. We were only one night in them that time, but it was a useful breaking-in experience, and hardened us a bit for the much longer spells, during which the cold was so intense that the rifles were frozen as they lay on the parapets, if care had not been taken to keep them well oiled after firing.

We got some fine experience and first-rate preparation as a nerve-steadier in carrying out the duties of "listening patrol." When night came we went out of our trenches and made our way to the front of the parapet, working in pairs. This work was both dangerous and ticklish, for we had orders not to fire under any circumstances, as that would have brought the German machine-guns on us; but to use only the bayonet in case we came across parties of the enemy.

The object of the "listening patrols" was to find out, if we could, the German working parties putting up barbed wire entanglements and doing other things for their own protection. One of the pair of men would lie down on the ground and listen, and the other would be on the alert, ready to report instantly any suspicious noise that was noticed. If the Germans were putting up barbed wire, it meant that they were quite exposed and good execution could be done amongst them by our machine-guns; on the other hand, if the enemy heard our "listening patrols" they would instantly open fire with machine-guns and rifles and anything that came handy.

Patrol work was very trying, especially on the intensely cold nights, when it was a hard matter to keep awake, and the man who was lying on the ground was almost frozen stiff.

This sort of work went on for several weeks—until about March, slushing about in the trenches, and often enough, when we went out of them at night we would fall, in the darkness, into trenches that were full of water. Sometimes men were in it up to the neck, and the only way to get your clothes dry was to let the heat of the body do it—a long business at times, when the body had very little heat to spare. There was no help for it, because the men who came to grief like that could not change at all.

Early in March we were digging trenches on La Bassée Road. This work occupied us for several nights, and though we did not at the time fully understand its meaning, we knew afterwards that the

51

trenches were meant for the massing of our men for the battle of Neuve Chapelle. These were reserve trenches, and in the open; the consequence being that they were exposed to the German fire, and the digging was very dangerous work. We used to get as many as a dozen casualties in a company while digging, and one spot became known as "Suicide Corner," because of the heavy losses there. Of course, the digging was always done at night; but digging means making a noise, and whenever the enemy heard a noise they went for the place it came from.

It was at "Suicide Corner" that I made my first real acquaintance with the horrors of war. As usual we had gone out to dig. We had been taken to our allotted place by the Engineers, every other man carrying a spade, and our rear being brought up by four or five stretcher-bearers. It was obviously to our interest to dig as hard as we could, to get shelter, and we went at it with a will, being pretty well massed.

There was a man quite close to me, digging for all he was worth. Suddenly he went down, and I felt sure that he must have been shot, because the Germans, doubtless hearing our digging, had opened rapid fire on us. I soon found that the poor chap had been shot through the chest, and I went to fetch up our stretcher-bearers. They came, and a doctor came, and the man was carried to the shelter of a neighbouring hedge, where the doctor and the stretcher-bearers did everything they could for him, by the light of an officer's electric pocket-torch; but he had been mortally wounded in the chest, and he died at the hedge side, in the darkness which was lit only by the light of the torch and the flashes of machine-guns and rifles. The poor fellow was covered up and put on a stretcher and carried back to the billet.

This was the first man I had seen killed in action, and it made a very deep impression on me, especially as it happened at night. That picture of the dying soldier under the hedge, with the doctor and the ambulance men striving by the light of the little torch to save him, will, I think, remain in my memory when many of the bigger happenings of the war have faded and are almost forgotten. It is an early and a very sorrowful impression of the days that came just before the beginning of the furious battle of Neuve Chapelle.

No one who was in those Neuve Chapelle operations will ever forget the massing of the British forces for the fight. The whole countryside was alive with troops of every sort, and there was the incessant rumble of gun-carriages, ammunition-wagons and heavy motor-lorries, and the tramp of hosts of men on the march. There was a great deal of inevitable noise, but at the same time a sinister and impressive quietness. There was the feeling in the air that something very big was going to happen, and everybody felt on the "edge."

The Kensingtons went on in the night until we got into some reserve trenches, which there had not been time to finish properly. They were simply scoopings in the ground, with the earth thrown up on each side, a rough-and-ready sort of arrangement, affording very little cover and with not enough room for us to lie down—indeed, so shallow were they that when the bombardment began in the morning we were actually lying one on top of the other.

The bombardment which opened the battle of Neuve Chapelle began fairly early, and it is no exaggeration to say that when the immense number of guns began crashing it was hell let loose. The very earth shook, and no part of the country where we were seemed to escape from the shattering effects of the shells of every sort which were bursting all around us, a great many of them in the air. Some shells fell into the reserve trenches, and many of our fellows were hit.

The trenches in front of us were manned by two fine Line regiments, and these troops were ordered to advance towards the Germans and dig them out of their trenches. The Linesmen had a heavy task before them, but they began to carry it out most gallantly, and while they did so we came in for a very furious attack from the enemy's batteries, because, although they could not get at the advancing Regulars, we were well in the zone of their fire. We suffered severely during this bombardment, and were glad when the order came to rush to the trenches that the Linesmen had left and take their places.

To get to the trenches we had to rush over some fields, and as we dashed along we were under a heavy fire, which caused us serious losses, and those of us who reached the comparative shelter of the trenches were thankful when we were able to drop into them and so escape from the open ground. The thing to do was simplicity itself, and that was to get across the open space from one lot of trenches to another. There was no question of doing anything except look after yourself and carry out your orders; there was no chance of helping any one who fell—it was forward all the time, and those who went down had to be left where they fell.

Shells were bursting everywhere and the fragments were scattered all around the battlefield, and men were going down, killed or wounded, on every hand. It was through this real hail of fire that we reached the trenches which had been occupied by the two Line battalions, and then we saw a sight that I, at any rate, shall never forget—a spectacle, too, which proved how terrible the struggle was and how greatly the Regulars had suffered.

I talk of trenches, but no such things were left—the German gunners had smashed them out of all resemblance to ordinary trenches—and owing to one of those inevitable happenings of warfare some of our own British shells also had helped to complete the work of destruction.

The trenches had been blown in on all sides, and the barbed wire entanglements near them had been utterly destroyed, so that what we saw was a confused heap of ruins, or rather an area of shattered ground in which men had been killed and buried at the same time. The real horror of this part of the affair was to see the brave fellows who had done their best, and were now lying dead and shattered in the debris.

I soon had a very bad experience in the trenches that we had taken over, so to speak.

I and another Kensington had been allotted a firing position, and we were doing our best with our rifles when I suddenly became aware that my companion had come to grief. I looked round and saw that he was lying at the bottom of the trench—and I made the terrible discovery that his head had been blown completely off. I would not mention this circumstance except by way of trying to show what the whole of the trench warfare meant. This incident occurred in the open trenches; but a lot of the dug-outs were blown in with the men inside, which meant burial alive, and I know of one case in which seven men, so killed, were lying together, and that is only one instance of many of the same sort in this tremendous war.

When we got into the trenches that had been occupied by the two Line regiments we were ordered to take up a firing position, and the first thing we did was to try and restore the parapet and to make the trench serviceable, in case the Linesmen were driven back. At this particular time everything gave way to the chief business in hand, which was to fight, and only the stretcher-bearers were allowed to do anything for the men who fell. Here, again, every other man carried a spade, and those who had them had to set to work at once to put the trenches to rights again, as far as it was possible to do so. This work was being done very vigorously when it had to be dropped suddenly, because the order came that we were to advance right up into the village of Neuve Chapelle; and so it happened that we were rushed up just behind the spot where the Regulars had dug themselves in. We rushed up into the village and lay in the open, behind some ruined buildings.

The Germans had arranged a counter attack, and if this had come to anything we should have made a dash for the trenches, which were just in front of the village; but as it was we made for the village itself, or what was left of the place, for by this time there was nothing left but the ruins, and the whole region was an absolute shambles.

Before we made this rush the men of the Line regiments began to bring in German prisoners. These came in batches of fifteen or twenty, disarmed, of course, so that one or two British soldiers were enough for a batch. These prisoners looked as if they had had a terrible time, and, indeed, they said they had been through some dreadful experiences owing to our artillery, and that our guns had given them a shell for each yard of ground they held.

The German attack not having materialised, we were able to retire to the trenches and make them habitable. Before this could be done we had to get the wounded out and bury the dead. As a rule, we had dug a grave for each man, but now there were so many of the killed that we had to put the bodies side by side in long trenches, which we made just behind the line. Quite a cemetery came into existence there, and we did our best to make it nice and worthy to be the resting-place of those who had given their lives for their country.

There is one feature of this great war which has been lost sight of to some extent, and that is the tremendous call which has been made on the physical endurance of the men, quite apart from the ceaseless and excessive strain on the nerves and mind. I will give one illustration on this point.

On the night of March 10th, during the battle of Neuve Chapelle, the front line ran short of ammunition and the Kensingtons were ordered to take up a supply. First of all we had to load up with our little lot, and, as it was impossible to carry the ammunition in the cases, each man got a score of canvas bandoliers across his shoulders, in addition to his own kit and rifle, and he had to stagger along with this tremendous weight, the filled bandoliers alone representing about eighty pounds; so that with the rifle and standing kit each man carried a burden of considerably more than a hundredweight. That was bad enough, but matters were made infinitely worse by the fact that we had to go along a newly-made road, or rather track. This road had been constructed by the Gurkhas, by the simple plan of putting bricks down almost anyhow—there were plenty of bricks handy from the ruined buildings all around us; so that the road we had to take was rather like the huge teeth of an enormous saw, for there was no steam roller to flatten down the surface.

In the darkness, under constant fire, we staggered and stumbled along with our ammunition; but even the biggest and strongest amongst us could not do more than cover about a hundred yards at a time. If a man did that he was proud and thankful, and having got a bit of rest as best he could—and that was by hunking up and resting on the rifle, for if a man had really got on to the ground he would have been hard put to it to rise again—we forged slowly ahead.

We had been ordered to take the ammunition into a house that was battered, but was more whole than the rest—it was really only a skeleton of a building—and having reached the house we very gladly dumped our bandoliers down in the garden. To reach the garden was quite a simple matter—all we had to do was to dash through a big hole in the side of the house, made by artillery fire, and I give you my word that we lost no time in shedding our burden of bandoliers.

It was a most exciting little performance from start to finish, yet it put a terrific strain on every man who took part in it—load yourself up with more than a hundredweight of stuff and see what it feels like; then you will partly realise what we had to go through— and the excitement was by no means ended when we reached the garden in the darkness, because just as we were getting rid of the bandoliers a shell crashed into the house next to us and smashed it to smithereens, a lot of our chaps being fairly smothered in the flying bricks and rubbish.

That was a night, and one that I shall never forget.

There seemed every prospect that we should be fairly mopped up, and when the order came for the N.C.O.'s to take back the men in parties we lost no time in returning, as best we could, to the trenches. Shelling was going on all the time, and just by way of giving a finish to the performance something like thirty star-shells burst together, making the dark night as light as day and giving the Germans a chance to plump more shells into us as we got back. This hurrying up with ammunition to the firing-line is only one of many such things that have been done as part of the day's work by British soldiers at the front.

About two nights afterwards these two Line battalions of which I speak were relieved, and we took over their trenches. There were no dug-outs, or any such protections; the trenches were simply breastworks, and we had a very bad time when the wet weather set in, as it did.

When we took the trenches over they were in an unfinished state, and we set to work at once to complete them. One night, or rather about two o'clock in the morning, I was working on the top of the back parapet, with my head and shoulders showing, and half asleep, for I was dead tired. Suddenly the Germans sent up about fifty star-shells, which burst in the sky and made the darkness as light as day and showed us up as clearly as possible. Instantly the enemy opened rapid fire on our trenches and swept us with machine-guns, the bullets whistling over the parapets.

I was roused as swiftly as if the réveillé had sounded—perhaps faster, because there are no whizzing bullets when the bugles blow—and I well remember that I wriggled and rolled sideways. I knew that the darkness had become as light as daytime and that the German fire was peppering us, and that the best thing to do was to get out of it as rapidly as I could. So I fell flat, then lay still, then rolled into a trench as best I could. I remember—so soon do we get accustomed to war—that one of our chaps growled, "Why don't you go a bit farther, then you could go through an opening!" Fancy a chap picking and choosing a landing-place when he was clearing out from shell-fire! I knew that in rolling and falling like this there was a risk of landing on top of a fixed bayonet, as some of our fellows did, but I cheerfully took that chance in my eagerness to get under cover.

After this we polished up our bayonet work and went through a lot of routine, at the end of which we were told that we were to take the offensive and that some Regulars were to do the support work—a proud position for Territorials. So we filed into a front trench and relieved men who were only seventy yards away from the Germans, so that we knew we should not have far to rush when the real business came to hand.

I wish I could tell you of what happened on the glorious Ninth of May, when, according to all reports, the Kensingtons did so well and won so much praise from General Rawlinson; but I cannot go into detail, for I was hit at the start, and fell before the German lines were reached. I know that this particular fight began early in the morning, that it lasted all day, and that our chaps were practically surrounded. The order had come that we were to go for the Germans, and I was doing my bit in carrying it out.

We were rushing forward when I was shot through the chest and was knocked completely out. When this happened I was in a trench, and our chaps were cheering loudly, as if no such things as Germans existed.

The bullet that struck me had gone through my left lung, though I did not know this until later, and I had had a very narrow escape; but I did not at the time fully realise how close a call I had had.

After being shot I just managed to get back over the parapet, and I was bandaged up and kept going for the time being.

I felt pretty well until the alarm came that the Germans were starting on the gas tack, and then I wanted to be on the move. Respirators were fixed, and every preparation was made to meet the devilish device. For my own part, being shot and helpless, I naturally wanted to be out of it, so I beseeched the stretcher-bearers to carry me away, so that I should have, at any rate, a sporting chance.

"Will you try and get me out?" I said; "because I know that gas will finish me." And being good chaps two of them came, put me on a stretcher, and carried me down a communication-trench and into safety, under a constant and heavy fire, which lasted all that famous day.

I have been yarning long enough, though I could say a good deal more. By way of finish I will tell you of a little incident of sniping.

Sniping was going on all the time. In many places it was very deadly, especially where the green uniform of the snipers harmonised with the cabbages, so that the snipers could not be seen. We got used to the cabbage-patches whizzing bullets, but we were puzzled by some especially dangerous firing which came upon us from the rear. For a considerable time we could not make this out; then we discovered a haystack, and suspicion was aroused. We kept a strict watch, and made particular inquiry, and were rewarded at the end of it, by finding that what looked like an inoffensive haystack was a place of cunning hiding for a German marksman. This special rick concealed in its very heart a son of the Fatherland, who had been having a truly glorious time in potting us. He knew that he was certain to be discovered; but he went on sniping till we found him and put an end to his performance. He knew that his discovery was certain, and that discovery meant death; but he kept his game up—and he died game.

This was quite fair and square fighting, for sniping is legitimate. I cannot say as much for the German practice, which we fully proved, of using dum-dum bullets in their machine-guns. This they did by taking out the bullets as ordinarily used and reversing them.

CHAPTER VII

TEN MONTHS IN THE FIGHTING-LINE

[It is almost incredible that a man can endure a war like this for the best part of a year without a break; yet there are many British soldiers who have had that experience. At the outset these were mostly the old Regular troops who for efficiency and discipline were unrivalled in the world's armies. The story of one of these long-service Regulars—Private Frederick Woods, 1st Battalion Royal Irish Fusiliers—who served at the front for ten months and was then gassed and invalided home, is told here.]

I had ten months at the front with my regiment before I was invalided home, and I think that during that long period I saw every form of fighting except one, and I have just been reading about it. That exception is the use by the Germans of liquid flame, which they sprayed on French troops some time ago and are now sending on to the British. It is a devilish and cowardly device, but quite in keeping with the German method of warfare. The Germans don't understand the meaning of honourable fighting, and there is no cruelty and barbarity that they have not practised during the year of war that has ended at the time we are talking together.

It is natural enough that I should take my mind back to a year ago. How clearly I recollect that morning when I had just finished breakfast and opened my newspaper, and to my astonishment saw that war had been declared and that all Reservists were to report at once, without waiting for the official notice from the depot.

I was a Reservist of the Royal Irish Fusiliers, and had done seven years with the colours, so I at once went to my old home. I will confess that I was a bit downhearted, because my brother, also a Reservist, had come home, too, and he had the pain of saying good-bye to his wife, as well as to our parents. But we made the best of things, and it was the better for the two of us because we both belonged to the same battalion.

How many of us who assembled at Euston Station for the journey to our depot in County Armagh, Ireland, are left, I wonder? Not many, there cannot be, for the Royal Irish Fusiliers have suffered terribly in the war. The old soldiers assembled with brave hearts and were full of fun, and left Euston singing "Tipperary" in fine form. I well remember how much amused we were, when crossing in the boat, at a man who had come from Lancashire. He was wearing wooden clogs, and had a bottle of whisky with him; and he sang and danced and became particularly lively, and we thoroughly enjoyed his performance. At the depot we found our clothes and equipment waiting for us, and next day a big draft of us set out for England, my brother and myself amongst them. It was wonderful to see the draft and realise that here were fully trained soldiers, completely equipped, ready to take the field, and yet only a few hours ago many of the men were in civil life in various parts of the United Kingdom.

I had the strange experience of dealing with German soldiers before we left England, for a score of us were given ammunition and driven to Folkestone Harbour Station to meet a train of German Reservists who were trying to get away by a boat which was lying in the harbour, ready to take them to the Fatherland by way of Flushing. But the German Reservists didn't get off, and they had a big surprise when they saw us waiting for them. We searched them, of course, and found that several of the men were carrying arms. We took them to Christ's Hospital, the beautiful building in Surrey, and I suppose that they are still prisoners of war in England. These men were the usual type of Germans who were so often seen in London—waiters, and barbers, and so on, and I fancy that some of them were not sorry to be just too late to join the German Army. I cannot help thinking how different were these "reservists" to the long-service men who had rejoined the British colours.

I am not going into any details of the earlier part of the war; but I was not long before I saw a few more German prisoners on the other side. We had marched two days without seeing the enemy, then our scouts returned with three prisoners. The scouts told us that they had banged into the Germans, who were retreating fast, and had captured these three fellows. I was deeply interested in the prisoners, because they were the first German soldiers I had seen. They struck me as being somewhat miserable specimens, but that was perhaps because they seemed very hungry. They looked better when we had given them some biscuit, which of course we did at once.

Very soon after that I saw a farm which our artillery had hit, and which was in ruins and full of dead Germans. They had not had much of a chance against the British gunners, and I noticed that along the road leading to the farm ammunition was lying in heaps. It was a gruesome place to billet in; but in spite of the German dead we passed quite a comfortable night at the farm. Next day we were on the move again, and reached a river where a bridge had been blown up. This delayed us till the following morning, as our transport could not cross. But we found a way out of that trouble by taking the transport along a railway, and a rough, hard job it was, too, for we needed four horses and men with ropes to do the hauling, as the wheels kept getting stuck between the sleepers. But in spite of all the difficulties we got the transport across, and reached a town which the Germans had passed through; and we did not want telling which way they had gone, as we could see champagne bottles and wine bottles along the road for miles—drink which the Germans had looted from the town.

Drink and outrage and destruction marked the path of the German troops, wherever they had been, in those early unforgettable stages of the war, just as they did afterwards; though I believe that now, when they know that they are outcasts from civilisation, the Germans are disposed to mend their ways, if only to get better treatment when the final reckoning comes.

There comes into my mind as I talk the picture of a dreadful sight I saw near Armentières. We had reached a place and entered it, not knowing that the Germans were so near at hand, though we knew that we had them on the drive and that they were going away from us as hard as they could travel. Suddenly we came to a nunnery, where the nuns showed us the dead body of a little French boy, a mere child about five years old. A glance was enough to show that he had been bayoneted in the stomach, and it was clear that the cowardly murder had been done quite recently. One of our officers made inquiries of some nuns, and he was told that a drunken German soldier had killed the child. Can you wonder that when our eyes saw such dreadful evidence of German devilry and German cowardice, the Royal Irish Fusiliers, at any rate, made up their minds that whenever the chance arose the enemy should be severely punished? Nothing has been done by British soldiers in this war that has not been fair and square fighting, but I am glad to think that many a German coward and murderer has paid the penalty of some foul crime at the point of a British bayonet.

Even in the way of ordinary warfare many innocent women and children have been killed, quite apart from the large numbers who have been wantonly murdered by German brutes. In one village we passed through one of our men found a woman's head of hair, which had been cut off, and the body itself was found by civilians. The woman had been maltreated and murdered by the Germans, and on every hand there were signs of the enemy's ferocity and inhumanity. Buildings were in ruins and homes were wrecked, doors having been battered down so that the savage soldiery could wreak their maddened will on fellow-creatures and their belongings.

On every hand there was evidence of outrage. I went to a farm in this village to try and buy some milk and eggs. On entering a room which had a big fireplace, I saw in the corner of the fireplace an old man who seemed to be an idiot. A woman, whom I took to be his wife, and could speak broken English, told me that the Uhlans had taken him away, with his hands tied behind him.

"Why did they take him? What had he done?" I asked her.

She answered that the man had done nothing, but that the Germans had accused him of firing a shot. He had not done anything of the sort, for the shot had been fired by a French patrol; but in spite of his declarations, protests and appeals, the Germans beat the poor old fellow on the head with their lances and did their best to force him into a confession that he had fired. But he would do nothing of the sort, and at last they let him go—they would not have done that if they had not known that he was perfectly innocent. He managed to get back to his home, covered with blood and almost senseless, and the first thing that was noticed about him was that he had lost his memory. He very soon became the sorry spectacle I saw in the corner of the fireplace, an innocent man who had had the life nearly beaten out of him and had been maltreated into idiocy. It took me some time to understand the real point of the Germans' brutality—that they had let the poor old fellow loose and told him to run, and had battered him on the head and prodded him with their lances because he did not run fast enough. These are the soldiers who boast that what they have done in Belgium and elsewhere is nothing to what they would do in England if they got here. And for once I believe their boast.

I recall the sad case of another old lady I saw. She was crying bitterly, and when she was questioned explained that the Germans had taken her son away—ando he was never seen again. Like so many more of the inhabitants, he had fallen a victim to German "frightfulness."

If you turn from these sad cases—and I have mentioned only one or two that come into my mind—and try to tell of what was done to ordinary people because they happened to be in the war zone, words almost fail you; but I recollect that at one time we had been relieved by French Alpine troops and had entrained for St. Omer, where Lord Roberts died, while the guns were solemnly booming in battle.

We reached St. Omer and were resting on the square, when a German aeroplane came over and dropped two bombs, killing a woman and a child, but no soldiers. As soon as it was seen that this was happening, one of our own aeroplanes was sent up after the German. Up he went, in glorious style, and brought the baby-killer down; and when we saw it we cheered for all we were worth. The German dropped between the two firing-lines and was shot. We tried to make him a prisoner, but every time we made a rush to get him the Germans fired on us, not caring in the least about the fate of their own airman. The machine itself was shelled by us and burnt.

When we reached the Aisne we found that a bridge by which we were to cross was blown up; but our engineers soon repaired the bridge, which had not been destroyed properly, so that it was strong enough to carry us. Having crossed the river, three regiments went to the tops of the hills and entrenched—the Warwicks, the Dublin Fusiliers, and the Seaforths, our own regiment being left in reserve at the back of a village.

The French troops were on our left, in front ofo Soissons, and we used to see their artillery galloping across the plain with ammunition for the guns. The French use mules and not horses for their batteries, and once we saw some artillery galloping in fine style under German fire. When the guns were passing near us four shells landed amongst the limbers, but no one was hurt, and on seeing this we gave the Frenchmen a tremendous cheer, for luck, and they replied with cheers and wild waving of whips as they galloped away and nearer into the fire zone. I remember that day well, because on the night of it we had to go and bury thirty-five of our artillery horses that had been killed.

Next day was our turn for shell fire from the Germans. The shells landed right into us, but we were lucky—only one man was killed though several were wounded. We advanced up the hill, out of the way of the fire; but as we moved the enemy gave us shrapnel, and the shelling became so heavy that half-way up the hill we dug ourselves in.

While we were going up the hill, in short rushes, just like an ordinary field day, and without any confusion, an artillery corporal, whose name I do not know, showed splendid courage and uncommon strength in carrying several of our men to a hospital which the Germans were shelling. For his bravery he received the French Médaille Militaire.

Our transport had a very rough time, for out of fifty horses no fewer than forty-two were killed or had to be shot. Twenty men were picked out, myself amongst them, and sent back some distance for new horses, and I am glad to say that we returned safely with the animals.

I was then put on guard over a bridge which waso a special favourite with spies. They were always trying to get through, but in most cases they failed, and being caught and found out, there was no waste of time in shooting them, after trial by court martial. After being relieved at this place by French Alpine troops we entrained for St. Omer, the place I have mentioned, and from St. Omer we were rushed in French motor lorries for about sixteen miles, to a village where we rested for the night. Next morning we were told that the Germans were on a hill six miles away.

I shall never forget that day, because it rained in torrents, and it was a sodden regiment that trudged through the mud and mire and swished across drenched fields. It was not exhilarating, but we were soon warmed up by the German fire. We were ordered to lie down, and down we lay in a field of swedes, so we fairly flopped into beds of mud and water, just about completing our discomfort.

The rain was pattering down like tiny bullets, but we also got a shower of the real things, and you could hear the bullets "zip" into the leaves of the swedes. It was intensely trying and very miserable to be in such an exposed place, and we were glad when the order came to fix bayonets, ready for a charge. We fixed bayonets, but had to wait some time before the order to charge came; then we heard the word we wanted, and up we rose and off we went. The firing became hotter than ever, and several of our men were killed and wounded before the top of the hill was reached.

There was not much commotion as we advanced, but somewhere a Seaforth Highlander was playing bagpipes, and the skirl helped the boys along.

We expected some stiff work when we reached the top of the hill; but when we got there we were astonished to find that the Germans had gone, taking their wounded with them. We were after the enemy so quickly, however, that they had to leave their wounded, who fell into our hands, and of course got exactly the same treatment as if they had been British soldiers. A hundred and three of the poor beggars had been left in a convent for the nuns to look after, so you may be sure that they had been well cared for before they became our prisoners.

The Germans at this stage were retiring rapidly, and we kept them on the run. We soon came to a little village, where we found that the Germans had put sandbags in the church tower and had planted a machine-gun in the tower. A French flag which was flying on the tower the day before had been dragged down by the Germans and torn to pieces. We looked upon the flag with sadness, for here again we had evidence of German brutalities—in their retirement the soldiers had maltreated the women, and they had battered down doors and smashed windows in their savage determination to enter houses. They accused the villagers of firing on them—though the villagers had nothing but a few old useless firearms, which we saw. In spite of this they declared that a man had fired on them, and they shot him. The body was taken away by a priest. These things, I can assure you, roused us up properly, and we put plenty of heart into our continued pursuit of the Germans; but they were flying so fast that they were very hard to catch.

We came up with them in the big town of Armentières, and were so close to them that as we entered the town our scouts came back and told us that the enemy were just leaving it at the other end. As we entered the town we were cheered enthusiastically by the French, who seemed to look upon us as deliverers, and so loaded us up with gifts of chocolate bread, matches and so on that we had to throw half the things away.

Going into Armentières on the very heels of the Germans was an exciting and dangerous performance, and as we advanced along the streets we went on each side, not knowing on which side shots would come from windows, but ready for anything that happened, as the men on one side had their rifles handy for any German that appeared on the other. This was a better plan than being on the look-out for trouble from the windows just above your head. Luckily not many shots were fired upon us at this stage; but we soon came to a farm where one of the most desperate little fights that I can call to mind took place.

We were wary in entering the farm, for we saw at once the sort of thing we had to tackle. There were four Germans concealed in a cellar the window of which was on a level with the ground, so they had full control of the yard and the entrance-gate.

Some of our boys, with Captain Carbury, went in and tried to persuade the Germans to surrender, but their answer to the coaxing was a volley which killed the officer and wounded the men. The captain was terribly mutilated, for he had been struck full on the body, not by an ordinary honest bullet, but an explosive bullet, and the men had been badly hurt. As they lay on the ground they cried for help, and all the time the Germans were firing on them and succeeded in hitting them on the legs and shoulders. Two of our men, brave fellows, volunteered to try and save their wounded comrades, and they dashed into the yard, only to be shot and killed as soon as they entered. One of these fine chaps was Lance-Corporal Shield, but I do not know the name of the other.

It was useless to waste further life in the attempt to get the Germans out of their strong little position, from which they could fire without making themselves targets, so our officer sent for some engineers to undermine the farm and blow it up. The Germans were warned what was going to be done, and were called upon to surrender. This they refused to do.

During that night the engineers were working like moles, and

65

I didn't envy the feelings of the Germans who were trapped in the cellar, nor was there any pity for them next morning when the engineers finished their work.

There was a crash and a flame and a shaking of the ground—and when, later, things having settled, we went to see what had happened we found one badly damaged German hanging over an iron girder on to which he had fallen after being blown up. We made a prisoner of him. His three companions had been killed, and we saw that they had been blown to pieces.

The Germans by this time had received big reinforcements, and they entrenched themselves strongly. We entrenched as well, and a warm job it was, as bullets used to whistle past us constantly.

We were in these trenches thirty-seven days before we were relieved, and long, hard days and trying nights they were, putting an uncommonly severe strain on everybody. It was almost certain death for a man to show himself, yet men had to show themselves, because water had to be fetched and rations had to be brought up to the trenches and taken in. Whenever it was possible to do so advantage was taken of the darkness; but we could not always wait for night, and during the daytime some splendid acts of bravery were seen.

I will tell of one particular instance, because the man will be always remembered with pride by the Royal Irish Fusiliers—his valour won for him the Victoria Cross. This was Private Robert Morrow, an Irishman, who literally did not know the meaning of fear. One day we badly wanted some water, and this was to be had only from a farm which was some distance away. To reach the farm it was necessary to leave the trenches and cross open ground, exposed to the German fire, which was very deadly because we were so near the enemy's trenches. These were only about 600 yards away, and not more than 300 yards away were some snipers, in a farm in front of the trenches.

Morrow volunteered to fetch some water, and taking an empty two-gallon stone rum-jar he started on his perilous journey. As soon as he was seen after leaving the trench the Germans did their very best to pot him; but they missed every time, and Morrow reached the farm, filled his jar and began his trip back. And a hard business it was, for a jar like that will hold about fifty pounds' weight of water, then there is the jar and the awkwardness of carrying it when the carrier has to duck and dodge over every yard of the ground. But Morrow was a splendid hand at the game, and he actually managed to reach the trench in safety and was on the point of dropping into it with his precious water, and we were just ready to give him a wild Irish cheer. But at this very moment crash came a

66

German bullet, and the rum-jar was smashed to pieces and the water rained on the ground and was lost.

Morrow was the sort of chap who can't be beaten. Instantly he volunteered to go back to the farm with water-bottles. What can you do with such a man but let him have his way? We handed over the water-bottles, quite a festoon of them, and having slung them round him Morrow left the trench for the second time and began to make his way towards the farm.

As soon as he left the shelter of the trench he drew the German fire on him, and he was under it all the way to the farm, where he filled the bottles, and all the way back. This time he reached the trench safely and dropped into it, bringing the water with him and escaping every German bullet that was meant to kill him. He was a plucky kid and we were proud of him. And the regiment will be proud of him for all time—I say will be, for like quite a number of the heroes who have won the Cross Morrow has been killed.

Now that I am talking of him I recall the fact that only the day before he was killed he went to a well for water, and had a remarkably narrow escape from an odd sort of death—not a soldier's end at all. The Germans had blown the farm to pieces, but there was a lonely chimney-stack standing. When Morrow went to the ruined farm a high wind was blowing, and just as he was passing the chimney a strong gust brought it down in a heap at his very feet. Heo escaped by just a few inches from being killed and buried in the heap of masonry.

It was on April 12th that Morrow actually won his Cross. At that time we were near Messines, and the trench warfare was being carried on with great energy on both sides. Shell fire from the Germans was shattering and wrecking some of our own trenches, so much so that British troops were being buried alive in some places.

Several soldiers had been knocked out by shell fire and buried in the fallen earth. You can easily imagine what it means—men are in a trench, which is really a sort of vast open grave, and shell fire shatters the earth which is around and simply buries the men. So it happened on the 12th of April, and Morrow saw and knew it. Just as he had acted when he went and filled the rum-jar and our water-bottles with water, so he acted now—he gave no thought to himself. Out he went, not once, but many times, into a bullet-swept zone, till he reached the trenches which had been knocked out of shape by German shells, and in the rubbish of which his comrades were lying buried and helpless. He dug them out and pulled them out, and one by one he brought the senseless fellows into safety. That was the deed for which Morrow got the Victoria Cross; but in reality he had won the honour time after time. He was killed at "Plug Street," as we called the place. A piece of shell struck him on the head and he died immediately.

The most extraordinary things happened to some of our fellows, and there were escapes from death or capture so strange that you could not credit them unless you saw them. I will mention one particularo incident that comes into my mind. I saw one of our motor ambulances going along a road. There was nothing unusual in that, of course, because we have many motor ambulances and there are many roads, but in this case the road led straight into some German trenches. Before it was possible to do anything or raise an alarm the driver had blundered into the very midst of the enemy, and there he was, with his ambulance, just about as much amazed to see the Germans as they were to set eyes on him. They ought, of course, to have bagged both the driver and his vehicle; but he sprang down, restarted his engine and began to run away. The Germans pulled themselves together, and every man who could bring a rifle to bear fired on the retreating ambulance; but luckily the driver had a fair lot of protection, and though hundreds of bullets struck the bonnet of the car not one of them touched him, and he got safely away and went on his journey. It was a remarkable escape, and all who saw it were glad that the plucky chap got so well out of the trouble which had followed his mistake.

One night I was on sentry in the trenches when the sentry next to me gave the alarm. He had no sooner done that than he saw something crawling over the trenches. He did not waste a second—he lunged out with his bayonet, and then found that he had driven it into a German's shoulder. The German was made a prisoner, then it was discovered that he had lost his way in the dark and had got into our trench. When we searched him we found that he had a revolver and a long knife; but he was miserably clad, his feet being wrapped up in newspapers, as he had no socks. He said he was glad to be captured.

Our chaps sometimes make the same mistake—a very easy one, as the German trenches were so close to our own. Two of our men went, one dark night, to get some hot tea in dixies. On their return they got into a communication trench and lost their way; but at last, thinking they were home again, they shouted down a trench, "Hi, Bill, take the tea!"

Instantly bullets were flying around them, and realising that they were not back home at all, but had reached an enemy trench, they dropped the hot tea on the Germans, then ran for it and got safely off.

I had been a long time at the front before I was detailed to go back with the transport and bring up the officers' rations every night. We used to gallop as hard as we could till we came to a bridge, which the Germans could see and did their best to smash with shells. There was a sharp turning which a priest had called the "Devil's Corner," saying it was worse than hell because of the continual shelling. We were forced to take this road, because it was the only way to reach the trenches.

At night the Germans threw a searchlight on the "Devil's Corner," and as soon as ever they saw us appear they shelled us, sometimes as many as four shells coming together; but we dashed on so furiously that they could not get us, nor did they catch us when we ran the gauntlet coming back, though they used to get an average of a wagon a night. In addition to this deadly corner we had three burnt villages to tackle; but we were always lucky, and our men did not come to grief.

We used to go right up to the trenches, only about twenty-five yards from them, with the horses and wagons, and there was one specially dangerous spot which had to be passed. This was where there was a gap in a hedge, which the Germans knew of quite well and could see. They knew that at night our troops went to the gap to get water, and so in the daytime they trained machine-guns on the spot, and when darkness came they blazed away in the hope of wiping some of our men out. I have known these guns whirr for five minutes without a break, sending out a fire so horrible that nothing could live under it. We lost several men at this gap, and were forced to make an opening in the hedge somewhere else.

We got into reserve trenches, and here it was that a "whistling Willy," which is our nickname for a small German shell, went clean through a Seaforth and then killed one of our own men in the trenches. The shell passed through the Highlander intact, and did not explode until it reached the trenches, a circumstance which shows the amazing performances of projectiles in this war. You never know what they will do. At another time one of our chaps, named Steel, was having his hair cut, when a shell exploded near him and a piece of it, six inches long, like a needle, struck him through the heart and killed him on the spot.

The winter was a very rough time for us, as we could not keep the water out of the trenches, and we often had to sleep standing up, during a four days' spell in the trenches. Often enough, at the end of one of these hard spells, we were intensely disappointed because we could not be relieved, owing to troops being moved elsewhere, and we were forced to stick it for an extra four days; but we did not forget to make up for it when we were out, although we had to march a few miles to our billets to rest, and even then we were not free from shell fire.

By the time I had been at the front seven months I think I had seen almost every phase of this tremendous war; but I had yet a lot to learn of what the war means, and I began to learn afresh when we got to Ypres and later on had a dose of poison-gas.

None of the sights I had seen were to be compared with what we witnessed in the famous and beautiful old city, which the enemy had reduced to ruins. They had used shells of every sort, and I saw many evidences of the havoc and death that had been brought about on innocent people.

There was one house, on the left-hand side of the Museum, the home of a poor-class person, which was in ruins. I noticed this specially, as many of us did, because from the ruins there peeped some tiny feet—one of the most pitiful sights I ever saw. We made inquiry and found that a gas-shell had come, shattered the house, and killed and buried in the wreckage the father and mother and three children—a whole family of five, and it was the little feet of the smallest child that we saw amongst the debris. There was nothing for us to do but march on, and become more grimly determined than ever to fight and smash the enemy who had done these things. In cases like these we cannot stop to do anything; but there is the comfort of knowing that our fatigue parties will come up and give decent burial, and that the service will be conducted by a priest of the same faith as the slaughtered victims.

It was on April 26th that the gassing by the Germans began, and we had a repetition of the diabolical business on the 27th and 28th. We were1 quite taken aback by this development in the warfare, and as we were not prepared for it, not having even respirators, we suffered terribly. The men who got a full dose of the poison died an awful death, turning black in the face and foaming at the mouth, the buttons on our tunics turning rank green; while those who were only half-gassed reeled about like drunken men. I was lucky enough to be amongst the only partially gassed, but what with that and my ten months at the front I was pretty well worn out and was invalided home.

I have said that I have seen every form of fighting except one—the liquid fire. I have certainly been under every sort of fire but that, and I don't think I am saying anything unsoldierly in admitting that the fire I love best is the fire we left behind in dear old England.

CHAPTER VIII

A GUNNER AT THE DARDANELLES

["Next I come to the Royal Artillery. By their constant vigilance, by their quick grasp of the key to every emergency, by their thundering good shooting, by hundreds of deeds of daring, they have earned the unstinted admiration of all their comrade services." That is the tribute which General Sir Ian Hamilton paid to the gunners in his despatch describing the operations in the Gallipoli Peninsula—a document which is the story of a noble failure. Little has been told of the doings of the artillery, but we can realise what they did from this narrative of Gunner John Evans, 92nd Battery, Royal Field Artillery, who was included in the vast number of soldiers who were invalided home through sickness.]

I was in India with my battery when the war broke out. I had been in the country for seven years, and much as I liked it—I thoroughly enjoyed my soldiering there—I wanted to be off to the front. But I was kept in India for six months, training men to fight the Germans, and so doing my bit in that way. Then I came to England, where my battery had a splendid time because the people were so kind; and after that very pleasant change I was off to the Dardanelles, and went right into a fair hell of fighting. You can imagine a lot as a soldier, but no flight of fancy would ever have made you picture in your mind the things that actually happened. It is all over now, and some of us in hospital have time to think of the brave fellows who are resting in the Peninsula. They could not do what they were set to do, because that was beyond the power of ordinary man; but they did more, I think, than any other troops in the world could have done. To any man who knows what the country and climate are like, and who saw the difficulties and endured the awful discomforts, it seems that almost miracles were performed; and of all the wonderful things none was more wonderful than the withdrawal from Gallipoli.

We went straight into the business. There was no beating about the bush over the job. We got there, to the famous Lancashire Landing at W Beach, and my battery was the first to land on Turkish soil. Looking back on the campaign makes you wonder that we ever got either in or out of Gallipoli.

71

When our transport got near enough for us to begin our landing operations we were treated to a fine view of the desperate fighting that was going on, to say nothing of being under fire ourselves from the Turkish guns, a proper preparation for the regular hell of fire that we were under when we actually landed ourselves.

The Turks had opened fire on our transport from the Asiatic side as well as the European side, and what was happening to our own ship was happening to a whole fleet of transports and all sorts of other ships. There were warships bombarding the enemy's position, and the din altogether was enough to stagger even a long-service gunner who thought he knew what noise meant.

This happened about half past ten in the morning. At that time the Lancashire Fusiliers were making their magnificent attempt to land, and I shall never forget their pluck and the way they stuck to their deadly job. They were being conveyed ashore in lighters, and the Turks—we could distinctly see them over the edge of the cliff, not a hundred yards from the foreshore—were pouring in a terrible fire at close range. Shells, too, were dropping from the batteries at Achi Baba, miles in the rear, with wonderful precision.

The Fusiliers' lighters could not get close to the beach owing to the barbed wire entanglements which had been fixed in the water, so the men were ordered to get out and wade ashore. This they began to do—and it was one of the most awful jobs that a landing party ever undertook.

I could see them quite well from our transport. Without a moment's hesitation the Lancashires clambered over the sides of the lighters and into the water they went, struggling to get ashore. It is hard enough to force your way through water at any time; put to that difficulty a heavy kit and rifle and ammunition, throw diabolical barbed wire in, and you will understand to some extent what it all meant.

As these brave fellows threw themselves overboard dozens of them were shot; a lot more were caught by the barbed wire, and as they were held helplessly, with flesh and clothing torn in their frantic efforts to get free, they were killed or wounded by the Turkish fire.

It seemed impossible for any of the Fusiliers to survive and get ashore, yet many forced their way through everything and landed on the beach, where they at once formed up roughly, and then without the slightest hesitation they charged up the face of the cliff, which looked to me almost as hard to scale as the side of a house.

As they scrambled up the cliff they were met by a more

murderous fire than ever from rifles and machine-guns, and numbers were killed or wounded. It seemed to me that for every man who reached the top at least four were killed or maimed. I could see the bodies rolling down the cliff-side on to the beach.

It was only a little band of Lancashire Fusiliers that managed to scramble and rush to the top of that terrific cliff—a few hundreds or so. They must have been exhausted; but their blood was fairly up, and with fixed bayonets they charged with such fury and success that the Turks were fairly taken aback, and I could see them giving way before our boys' cold steel.

Some of the Turks were throwing up their arms, and I could hear their shrill appeals for mercy; but the Fusiliers hadn't too much time to listen after the awful experience they had just gone through.

After they had been driven off the Turks made a counter-attack, and the Fusiliers, being a mere handful, were forced back to the very edge of the cliff and seemed in peril of going down it; but even then they re-formed and again rushed on the Turks with the bayonet and scattered them. Back again the Lancashires were driven, only to recover in the most amazing way and charge with the bayonet for the third time. And this seemed to settle the Turks, who cleared off.

While this thrilling fighting was going on, a sight that can never be forgotten by those who saw it, our brigade was getting ready to disembark. The infantry had had a hard enough business to get ashore; but ours was naturally a lot worse, for we had to tackle our guns and horses, as well as look after ourselves.

There were lighters alongside the transport, and into each of these we got two guns and eight horses, not easy work at any time, but hard now, with such a rush on and shells dropping all around us. Some of the explosions caused havoc amongst the horses, and several shells dropped near our lighter; but I am thankful to say that they were not near enough to do us much damage.

We were towed as near to the shore as we could get, and then we began the uncommonly hard and long job of getting the guns and horses ashore. The lighters were bobbing up and down and "ranging," owing to the run of the sea, and this unsteadiness made it very difficult to get the guns and horses overboard; but every officer and man worked with a will, and we did it. We got them out of the lighter and on to a strange kind of roadway that had been made in the water by putting sandbags tightly down. These sandbags "gave" a fair lot, of course, but we could not have done anything without them, for the wheels would have sunk too deeply in the wet soft sand.

When a gun was ready, from ten to sixteen horses were harnessed to it, and it took these and forty men on the drag-ropes to get one gun over the sandbag road on to the beach. We did our best, we strained every nerve, we were experts at the work, yet it was evening before the battery was ready for action. By that time we had got the guns on the level at the top of the cliff, about forty yards from the edge, after tremendous efforts by horses and men. I never saw such man-handling, even in India.

We had luck in the weather, for a heavy storm came on and the rain fell in blinding sheets. This, with the darkness, when it came, enabled us to take up our position without the Turks knowing of the fact.

Of course, while all this work of ours was going on the infantry were screening us in front. A constant and confused sort of fighting was taking place, and our men were mixed up with the enemy in furious hand-to-hand scraps. It was a regular bedlam, and so that nothing should be left in the way of trouble we were soaked to the skin. But we were so absorbed in the fighting, and so keen to get to work ourselves, that we did not give a thought to the drenching. We longed to get into action, but were kept back by the mixing up of our own men with the Turks, which made it impossible for us to open fire, because we should have killed as many of our own men as Turks.

We stood by till we knew that our infantry had driven the Turks well back, and then it was that the enemy got one of the biggest shocks of the day, for we simply let go at him with shrapnel at point-blank range. So well had we been handled by our officers that the first hint the Turks had of our presence was when we opened fire, and then the muzzles of our guns were almost in amongst them.

During the first few minutes of that tremendous excitement we did not bother much about the gun drill-book—I, for instance, was loading, setting fuses, ranging and doing any other work that came to hand. Despite this there was nothing whatever to grumble about in the way the guns were being served.

In the darkness we could not see what mischief we were doing, but we knew perfectly well that it must be enormous, because of the rapidity of our fire and the goodness of our shells; and when the daylightcame we had proof, for ahead of us were piles of Turkish corpses, men who had been killed by our shrapnel.

We went on firing till the Turks had been driven back in complete disorder. We kept the game up throughout the day, but the darkness prevented us from following the enemy's movements.

We, of course, had no observation-posts at that time, as there were no trenches available for the observation officers to get to know the results of our fire.

After this promising start things were fairly quiet till the small hours of the next morning, when the enemy counter-attacked with great fury. The Turks are rare good fighters, they knew the country, and they had German officers driving them on in the rear, brutes who shot them down without mercy time after time, as I saw with my own eyes.

There were some native troops on our right front, and these were so hard pressed that they were forced to give way.

A staff officer who was at hand realised instantly the serious state of the situation, as the line was broken, and he called on some of the gunners in our brigade to fill the gap.

About fifty of our men fell out at once. There were hundreds of rifles with fixed bayonets lying on the ground around us, and grabbing what they wanted of these, our men rushed up and joined in the fray, filling the gap and making good the broken line before the Turks could understand what was happening.

It was a smart little affair, and the enemy was driven back and had to scuttle for shelter to histrenches, where he was left for the time being, for our troops were utterly exhausted and a rest was necessary.

We were thankful for a bit of a break. It was not for long, but we took things fairly easily till just before midday, when another advance was ordered against Seddul Bahr, a village of great tactical importance some hundreds of yards away, on our right front.

Our brigade was ordered to get ready for action.

By this time we were better off than we had been, for we had established the necessary observation-posts, and so we were ready for anything that might happen.

At noon the order came to open fire, and we fairly rained shells into the village—hundreds of rounds of shrapnel—to help the infantry in their advance.

The Turks were just as ready as we were, and they started a bombardment both from Achi Baba and the Turkish forts on the Asiatic side.

Some of these shells were proper "duds," and they made us laugh. It was not necessary to be told that they were made in Germany, for they dropped harmlessly into the ground, without exploding; but of course there were lots that did burst and do mischief. Many of these dropped on to the beach down below, killing mules and causing losses amongst transport drivers and the men of the Army Service Corps. Owing to the luck of war we had not many casualties in our own battery, and the losses were nothing like what you would have expected from such a lot of firing from the Turkish guns.

But we had some sad losses, all the same.

Our major was amongst the few who were killedthat afternoon. He was in an observation-trench ahead, and was struck by a piece of shell which burst just near him. The news soon spread that he had been mortally wounded. He was most popular with the men, and as soon as they heard what had happened both officers and men rushed out to his post, to do what they could for him. But you can't do much for a dying man.

The major did not last long. His last words were, "Good luck, boys. Tell my wife I died happy."

There wasn't a dry eye amongst the men who laid him to his last rest.

They say that misfortunes never come alone, and it was all too true of us that day, for in the evening the colonel and the adjutant were done to death through German treachery.

We heard, but not till later, that a German came along a piece of enemy trench, close to the observation-post where the two officers were.

The German shouted, in quite good English, "All officers this way!"

The colonel and the adjutant, who did not suspect anything, got out on to the parapet of the trench, and instantly a hand grenade was thrown from an enemy trench quite close at hand. It exploded and killed both of them.

That's the sort of dirty trick which the Germans know so well how to play. They have a born gift for it—and that reminds me that the Germans who were with the Turkish forces were just as dirty and brutal in their methods as they are, by all accounts, on the Western front.

Looking through a pair of field-glasses, I have seen German officers during an attack by the Turks followthem with revolvers in hand—your German officer doesn't lead, he drives, having a precious regard for his carcase, and no earthly sense of honour—and I have seen them shoot Turkish soldiers who have fallen because they have been shot in the leg or have stooped to pick up a rifle which had been dropped. The German would be about a hundred yards in the rear, and would run up and deliberately shoot the prostrate man. I am talking now not from hearsay, but of what I have seen with my own eyes, and it does not help you to love the Germans.

I once saw a German prisoner, a fair specimen of the Prussian bully—he was a lieutenant—knock down a British sentry who had told him not to smoke in a part of the line where lights were prohibited. It was lucky for the bully that a British captain came along at the moment, or the fellow would have got the full force of the sentry's bayonet.

I heard Turkish prisoners say that the German officers treated the Turks with contempt, and it was a marvel that the Turks had not risen and slaughtered their so-called benefactors wholesale.

While on this point, I would like to say that as a fighter the Turk is a gentleman. We would go for them hammer and tongs in the ordinary way of scrapping; but ten minutes after it was over we would gladly shake hands with them—but we wouldn't do it with the Germans.

The dirty trickery that killed our colonel and our adjutant made our brigade swear that they would never spare the Germans when they met them in the way of fighting.

It was on the third day from the landing that we began the great advance which was meant to sweepthe Turks away from the Peninsula, but which failed through lack of men and ammunition.

On that day we moved our guns forward about three hundred yards, and took up a fresh position from which we could bombard the enemy with great advantage.

We were in that place for a fortnight, and during that time the infantry had many a desperate shot at Achi Baba, which was the Turkish stronghold. There were many attacks and counter-attacks, without much apparent advantage to either side; but matters favoured the Turks, who had been strongly reinforced and had prepared very fine defensive positions.

While we were here our brigade lost a fair number of men; but of course the infantry suffered far more.

I am proud to say that our battery was the nearest to the Turks, and was constantly in action.

One night we had a report that the enemy was going to attack us in great force, and on the strength of the report we had to retire to a safer position. We withdrew, not without a lot of grousing among the boys, and when we reached our new point we were heavily bombarded; but no infantry attack followed, as we had been led to expect.

There was a good deal more grousing next morning when we moved forward again, because the Turks began to shell us heavily as we went along the road. This showed how well informed they were as to our movements even since the previous evening; but luckily our losses amounted to only two or three horses.

The next day the great retirement of the Britishforces began, and the whole of our infantry fell back about two miles to a point which we had nicknamed Clapham Junction, because the two main roads in the Peninsula join there. The artillery did not retire, being supported on the right and in the rear by French troops and the heavy guns.

Everybody knows now that if there had been enough men and ammunition our infantry, instead of retiring, would have taken Achi Baba and driven the Turks out of the Peninsula. Let us hope that if we did not manage to do that, our tremendous losses were not in vain, and helped to spoil any plans for marching on Egypt and India.

Early in June we started business again with the Turks, and that was when the great battle of Krithia took place. This fight lasted two days, but we did not make much headway, as the enemy had got big reinforcements and had prepared a defensive position of enormous strength.

I had several narrow escapes from death during that great fight.

During a lull I was standing behind a bank with two or three other men, watching the enemy's artillery shelling a water-cart some distance away. The cart was going along a road, and we were wondering whether it would get clear or be blown up. While I was doing that, a shell burst right over us, making a horrible noise and peppering the air with pieces of shrapnel. I ducked my head instinctively, and so kept it on my shoulders. It was lucky for me that I did this, or I should have been killed, because the shell burst very low, so low that I got several shrapnel bullets through the back of my helmet, and the man nearest to me was seriously wounded by flyingbits of metal. The third man received a good shaking up, but was otherwise unhurt.

A day or two later I had an even narrower shave with death— one of those extraordinary bits of luck that are so common in a war like this, that you take them almost as a matter of course.

I wanted to be as comfortable as possible, and so I had started to make a dug-out for myself. I was under fire, but I did not pay much attention to that. I soon found that the ground I was working on was in a bad and insanitary state, so I gave up the job, and took myself off and began to try my luck at a place about fifty yards away.

I had just got to work on the new pitch when a huge high explosive shell dropped plump on the ground where I had been digging. It burst with tremendous force, and I was pelted with flying clods of earth and got a proper good shaking; but beyond that I was not hurt. But my first pitch was simply shattered, and if I had not cleared out I should have been blown to fragments, as I have seen many a fine chap blown in Gallipoli.

One of the very worst of my experiences was one day when I went to visit a chum who was on duty at the beach. I called at his dug-out, just as you might call for a chap at his home, and out he came, smiling, walking up to me to shake hands.

Just at that moment a shell of the enemy dropped short.

I was struck dumb with the shock. When I regained myself I looked for my chum, and a terrible sight met my gaze, for there he lay in little pieces.

I felt right cut up, as I had soldiered with him for years in India, and I was going to visit his home if wehad the luck to get through together. So you see we were so near but yet so far in a few seconds, and I am one of the lucky ones to be here to tell the tale. Out of the whole of the officers and men who came from India in my splendid battery, you could almost count those who are left on the fingers of your hands. Fighting and disease have taken nearly all of them.

More than once I was nearly "outed" by snipers; but I managed to keep a whole skin. It must be said in all fairness that the Turkish snipers were both plucky and resourceful—snipers were brought in who were found actually in our own lines; and once I was astonished to see a young and pretty Turkish girl brought in as a prisoner. She was a sniper, and had been hanging about our lines for a fortnight. There was no doubt that she was responsible for the death of several good men. We were greatly interested in this young lady, who was sent off to Tenedos.

These Turkish marksmen took every risk like good sportsmen, and we made their acquaintance right at the start, for when we were carrying out our desperate landing snipers were actually potting us from the beach, where they were covered with sand, so that it was almost impossible to see them. After that we got used to see snipers brought in who had painted themselves green, to match the trees and foliage, and others had decked themselves out with branches. It was funny to see some of the beggars, and as they had played a straight game we could not bear them any ill will. It was the Germans who did the dirty tricks.

Now for a few words on how I left the Dardanelles.

It was about July, when dysentery was at its worst, and quite half my battery were sick with it, all atthe same time. It came to my turn to get it, and I was very bad for about three weeks. At last I could stand it no longer, for I could not work without suffering awful pain—it was like two pieces of sandpaper rubbing together in one's inside, with much vomiting; so I was forced to report sick to our doctor, who was a gentleman and a brave man. He was very kind to me, and did all in his power for my benefit. But it was no good. I had to go to hospital. I thought this would be at a place a few miles away, and I was glad at the prospect of being out of the firing, which was awful to a degree, and to get some quietness; but I found myself at a beach hospital, which was composed of tents and was always under fire. Several shells dropped in on us, causing much damage and loss in life and material. So I was pleased enough when I knew that I was to go on board a hospital ship; gladder still when I knew that I was being carried to a place which was a little safer than Gallipoli, namely, dear old England. There was no room for us at two ports on the way home; but I didn't mind that. England was quite good enough for me.

We had a fine though sad voyage. It did one good to see the smiles on the faces of the wounded. Though they were in great pain, they were cheered with the thought that they were leaving a hell on earth for a turn in heaven.

That was the bright side of the case; the dark side was that our engines were continually stopped while one of our dear comrades was committed to the deep, where he could get the rest which he had so hardly won—but it was a godsend after what they had suffered.

I can assure the friends of those who are gone, that they were comforted in their last moments by the chaplain and nurses, and were given proper Christian burial as soldiers who had fought the good fight and had fallen in glory.

The brave nurses were like mothers with young children, and deserve the highest praise for what they did for us.

And now, through God's help, I am getting on all right, and awaiting orders for the front again, to do a bit more for King and country and to shame the slackers.

CHAPTER IX

THE "FLOOD"

[The following extract from a letter written by Corporal Guy Silk, 2nd Battalion Royal Fusiliers, has been very kindly placed at my disposal. It describes a phase of life in Gallipoli of which little or nothing has been published—the storms and floods with which our troops had to contend in the now abandoned operations.]

I have been wondering how you are getting on, and if you have been worrying over the absence of letters. There has only been one chance of sending a letter, and then I sent a card in an envelope to let you know that I was well. We have been through some terrible experiences since I last sent a proper letter, on November 25th.

On the 26th we had one more of those terrible storms, and suddenly, as I was mopping some water from the dug-out floor, a "tidal wave" burst in, and I just had time to seize the Company Roll, my diary and letters, Horlick's Malted Milk, and my rifle and bandolier. Then I climbed out of the dug-out, on to the parapet! The first, or rather second time I had done so (the first was to pick some tomatoes).

By this time the trenches were completely flooded, and the whole valley was covered with water ankle-deep. As the lightning flashed I saw a group of fellows near me, and they joined me on my mound. All around were similar groups. We laughed andpretended to be enjoying it, so as to keep our spirits up.

The water rose and rose, and when it was knee-deep we started off for a piece of higher ground we saw in the distance. We were in to the waist, and the current was tremendous. We settled down on this mound—the first one we saw proved to be just a clump of weed tops. The regimental sergeant-major joined us, but was nearly unconscious, and suffering with ague. I laid him on my lap, and there we stayed until daylight.

It was bitterly and painfully cold, and a curious sight too, when we first saw the huge mass of water and groups of wet men. I took the S.-M. on to headquarters, and there he was undressed and rubbed and wrapped in some dry blankets. Then our company sergeant-major was brought down, quite delirious, and Jackson and I took him on to the clearing-station.

It was fine to get on to higher ground out of the water. I reckon this walking saved me. I went back to the company, and found the water had gone from the ground in the valley, and the chaps were lying in hastily constructed breastworks behind the rear parapet.

The trenches were like canals, and were acting as drains. The Turks shelled a lot. This was on Saturday. In the evening and early morning of Sunday it snowed and froze, and on Sunday at daybreak we were ordered to find our way to the brigade "dump." At about midday we got some food and dry clothes. It was grand, after two nights and a day of sodden and frozen things.

We had a roll-call on Monday, and we were 63—onthe Friday afternoon we were 600 odd. I was made corporal—Baldion said I must be, so as to "help to hold the fellows together," and for a few days was acting company S.-M.!

We expected to go to Alexandria, but had to stay to drain the trenches. A big draft joined us, and did most of the work, our feet were too sore. (I spent one whole day rubbing feet—a savoury job, since baths are unheard of.)

On the Thursday after the "Flood" (everything dates from the "Flood" now) we went to find equipment, and the ground was covered with bodies.

We are back on the Achi Baba end now, but have not quite given up hopes of a rest, at least for the "survivors." I am orderly-room corporal now. Nearly all of us are employed at headquarters, so except for shells I am pretty safe, as we don't have to make advances.

We have had no mail since before the "Flood," but hope to get one soon. Please tell Aunt — I received and enjoyed her parcel (some was lost, buried when the trench fell in), and explain why I haven't answered to thank her for it. Let every one know I am still alive in spite of the long silence. We heard to-night that no mail is leaving for three weeks from to-morrow. The sketch-book has gone. I found it, but it was "done."

We had a busy time when the "Flood" had abated, and I was continually taking my section out, digging up rifles and equipment, and we were all able to make up our losses in the way of shaving apparatus, knives and forks, etc. It was hard work, as the trench bottoms are knee-deep in mud. We wore waders.

CHAPTER X

THE BELGIANS' FIGHT WITH GERMAN HOSTS

[It is hard, in language, to express the thoughts that come to one in contemplating the achievements of the Belgian Army at the outset of the war. Undoubtedly the coming sure defeat of Germany is largely due to the valiant stand which was made when the would-be all-world conquerors overran and ravaged a little, beautiful and inoffensive neutral state. The knell of Prussian doom was sounded first on Belgium's battlefields. It was believed that at the utmost Belgians could only make a pretence of fighting; but the little army of our brave ally defied and held at bay the braggart hosts of Germany in an almost incredible manner. What happened in those fateful days, which seem so far and yet in reality are so near is told by Soldat François Rombouts, of the 8th Regiment of the Line, Belgian Army.]

I was in the Belgian Army before the war broke out. I was a conscript of the 1913 class, and went to my regiment from the sea. For five years I had been crossing the Atlantic in liners sailing from Antwerp—and how beautiful it was in the summer-time on the blue sea, with the hot sun shining; and how hard and cold in the winter, peering into the grey gales from the crow's-nest! I loved the sea, and I loved my regiment, especially when I had my rifle in my hands and with my keen sea eyes I could make out the Germans and use them as targets. I do not know how many I shot—I hope and believe a big number—because when they fall it may not be always to your own bullet. But I saw very many of them fall beforeI was wounded and had to lie in bed for sixteen weeks, helpless, like a child.

Look at my right arm. Here, on the inside, a bullet went in. If it had been an ordinary bullet, like the one you show me—you say the cartridge was given to you by a British Guardsman who was at Landrecies and carried it there with him?—it would have gone through the arm and made only a little hole, which would soon have become well; but the bullet was explosive. See, here at the entrance is the small scar; but at the outside of the arm there is this long and ragged blue mark, because the bullet that struck me was what you call a dum-dum. Feel the wound, it does not hurt me now. That hardness is bone. It was carried away from the flesh and broken, and there it has set and will remain. For many weeks my hand was like this—a bunch, you call it?—because I could not open it out. I was hurt in other ways also by German fire; but I am young—only twenty-two years—and very strong, and I may yet again go back to the Belgian Army. If I do, and we get into Germany—as we shall—for every Belgian life that has been taken we shall take one German, and more; for every Belgian home that has been destroyed we shall burn or destroy one, and more, and for all the innocent women and little children and helpless old men that have been murdered we shall make them pay in German soldiers and in German soil.

I have my mother and sisters still in Belgium, where the German beasts are; and I do not know the truth of them. I pray that they are well; but if I learn that they have come to harm I will never rest until I have had my revenge in Germany. All Belgianswill tell you the same as that. How can it be otherwise when they have seen what I have seen—their country run over and beaten down and taken by these German hosts, who have swarmed over it like dirty beasts and fouled it?

How well I remember that night in Antwerp when the war broke out! It was eleven o'clock and the church bells were ringing.

That was the sound of war.

Several days we had been out of barracks, enjoying ourselves; but this night they would not allow us to go out.

My mother and sisters and brothers came, crying. They said, "The Germans will kill you!" But I said, "Shut up! It will not be so. Besides, I am a single man, and so I do not care. It is not as if I had a wife and children." So they were comforted, and I made myself happy by myself.

We were singing and whistling and dancing all night in barracks; then in the early morning we marched to Brussels, and after being there two days we were ordered to take the train to go to Liège, to keep the Germans back, and as we went along the people shouted, "Good Belgians! Good Belgians!"

We went by train to Liège, fifty miles away. We had got the orders we were waiting for in the evening—the orders to stop the Germans. If we could not stop them there, we were told, they would get through. And how true it proved!

We were in the train all night, singing and whistling, and all what we can do in a train to make soldiers happy.

The regiment that had gone before my own regiment was fighting. We had gone as reinforcements,and when we got to Liège at four o'clock on that August morning and got out of the train, fighting was going on.

I saw the Germans at once—we went straight into the street from the train and fought them.

We were excited, yes, but not afraid. They had come into our little country, where they had no right to be, and our only wish was to drive them away.

We rushed from the train with our loaded rifles. I did not know Liège. It was all strange to me; but all streets are much the same, and it was enough that the Germans were in them and must be driven out.

We fired on them, and they retired; but only a little way and for a little while, because there were so many of them. And in the evening they came back.

We fought them in the streets when they came, and we rushed into the houses and shot them from the windows and doorways.

Even now, so soon, I learned the truth of what I had said to my weeping mother in the barracks at Antwerp. She said, "The Germans will kill you!" and I told her, "No. I am not afraid of anything. The Germans cannot kill me!" And they did not—not then, and not later, though I was shot in the right arm with an explosive bullet and afterwards in the right foot, of which I will tell you.

I do not know whether I killed any Germans at Liège, but I hope I did. You could see them falling over, but could not say who killed them.

We hated them because they had come into Belgium.

We were fighting all night, the rifles crackling because of the constant firing of the magazines.

We chased the Germans into the fields outsideLiège. We got at stragglers with the bayonet, and we brought fifteen prisoners in. How amusing it was when we caught them! They said, "Oh, my Belgian brother!" We left them with contempt, and looked after other ones. Then, when we had got them, they were sent to the station and so to Antwerp.

The Germans came on in such strength that we could not stop them; but in spite of all their guns and regiments we held Liège for twenty-four days. We had only 300,000 Belgians in our army, and the Germans had about a million; but I would not run away from fifteen Germans myself. The Belgians called the Germans "swine," and said, "we will be giving the Germans one presently!"

And we gave them one.

We went into the trenches, and the Germans were bombarding us and smashing the place up. We did as much as we could to keep them back.

Houses were smashed and everybody seemed to be killed or wounded. The shells came on top of you and spread out like an umbrella. A lot of my friends were killed and fell over in the trenches.

When we were in the trenches a man near me was not happy, because he was married and his thoughts were with his wife and children and home; but when we were going on firing I said, "Look! A German has fallen over again!" And then he was happy. He was married and I was single, and that made the difference.

If you had your friend in the trenches you did your best for him, because you liked to take your friend home again; but many friends were left in the trenches.

Did I see General Leman, the defender and heroof Liège? Oh, yes. General Leman was a good man. He came round and saw the soldiers and talked to us and made us happy.

I do not know how many we lost in Liège. We had a lot wounded and killed and missing; but we only knew this from the newspapers.

We were on duty in the trenches for twenty-four hours, then we were relieved. At the end of the twenty-four days for which we held Liège we went to Anden, ten miles away. We retired in the daytime, without any fighting, and were in Anden about fifteen days. We never saw the Germans there.

And now I became a motor cyclist, which gave me many adventures and exciting journeys. I was with a friend, a motor cyclist also, and we were reconnoitring near Anden. We saw a big house, a château, standing in its own grounds, with trees. They are beautiful and peaceful houses, and you saw many of them in Belgium before the war.

"There are some Germans here!" my friend said. We looked and listened, and what he said was true. There were Germans in the château, but how many in number we did not know.

We hurried away to our officer and told him, and he sent three companies of soldiers to attack the château. How well they marched up, and how from behind the trees and other points of shelter they fired upon that big house in the trees, with the Germans making themselves happy in it.

I and my friend had acted as guides to the companies, and now we saw the Belgian soldiers firing upon the château, and the surprised Germans rushing to the windows and doors and behind the trees to fire back.

It was a furious fight, and it lasted for two hours. Then we got the house—the Germans ran away, and we took it and occupied it. But next day the Germans came back in stronger numbers and retook the château; and the day after that we once more got the house and killed all the Germans. We knew that we could not hold it long, because we had not enough soldiers, and when we had been at the château for about four hours, and the Germans came up stronger than ever, we had to leave. We had not had many losses—two or three men killed. One was shot through the heart, and another was mortally wounded and lived a few hours.

There is a river at Anden, and when we retired we had to cross a bridge. When we had crossed the bridge we blew it up, so that the Germans should be delayed in pursuing us. Then, when we were retiring, and had seen the bridge destroyed, we were made unhappy because we saw that on the other side of the water, which was now the German side, there was a company of Belgian infantry, which could not cross.

It was terrible and sad. What was to be done? How were our comrades to be saved, to come to us, to be kept from capture or killing by the Germans?

The commander of the company was quick to think and act. He knew that at Namur there were some boats, three or four of them. He ordered a cyclist to go and have the boats sent to Anden, so that the men could cross. And the cyclist went. It seemed so long before the boats came; but they appeared at last, and the soldiers got into them, crowding five and six in one small boat, and then being rowed over the river. All the time the Germans were firing on the company from the big hills which are there; butwe could not fire back, and all we could do was to watch our comrades on the other side of the river, walking about and eagerly waiting for the boats. They tumbled into the boats and came across the river to us, and we shouted and laughed when they were near enough for us to get at them, and to help them to jump on to the bank and to say defiance to the German bullets.

There is a railway tunnel at Anden, and we were ordered to go to it. We went. There is a big wood at the tunnel, and from this wood there came a party of Uhlans, fifteen of them, commanded by a lieutenant.

Three or four Belgians fired on the cavalry, who were taken by surprise. The lieutenant was shot in the side, next his heart, and he fell from his horse. The soldiers went up to him to make him prisoner of war, but he did not want to be taken, and he fired on them with his revolver. So it was necessary for them to shoot him, and they did.

When he was killed four soldiers carried him on two rifles, one under his back and one under his legs, to the major of the Belgian battalion, who ordered that he should be buried. So a grave was dug and the lieutenant was buried, and planks were put over him, and he was left there to his rest, and we attended to the German wounded.

After what happened by the railway tunnel we were ordered to make trenches; but the Germans came up and forced us to retire to Namur, an old city and fortress.

We saw many refugees who were flying from the Germans, who had come and stolen their land and plundered it and overrun it like dirty beasts. There were old men and women and children, and it was pitiful to see them; yet it made us fiercer in our fighting with the Germans.

Near Anden I saw a column of refugees, a little line of about thirty-five people, and at the head of them was a man dressed like a tourist, with a soft hat, breeches and leggings. He was looking under trees and all around him, as if taking care of the refugees.

Then, when we had seen this tourist, a boy came up to me on a bicycle, and said, "There is a German spy!"

I called my corporal, and instantly we had soldiers searching in the trees and fields and everywhere; but we did not see another trace of the "tourist," who was the German spy, though we did not suspect it when we saw him leading the refugees like a shepherd leads his flock.

That was sad, to miss him so; but another spy I got at Namur. I saw a man standing amongst the trees, dressed in civilian clothes. He was about fifty-nine years old and had long whiskers, such as you see on many tourists.

I went up to him as he was standing by a tree. I was alert, for I was reconnoitring and expected things to take place.

Before he could understand me and be ready to explain, I rushed at him and had him by the arms and held them to his back. My comrades came up and sent him with his long whiskers to the regiment. I do not know what happened to him. I hope they shot him.

I have here in my pocket an electric lamp with a bull's eye. It gives a fine strong light. No, this is not what I carried in Belgium, because I exchanged mine with an Englishman for his; but it is just the same. And with these pocket electric lamps we used to search the houses for Germans that were hiding from us. We would find them in dark corners and cellars, and when the light was snapped on them they would throw up their hands and cry, "Oh, my Belgian brothers!"

Then we would say, "Come out of it, and we will give you Belgian brothers!" But we always made them prisoners, and did not kill them. It was "Belgian brothers!" when death was on them, but in the trenches they called us "Belgian swine" and "little devils." We gave them "swine" presently.

We had been fighting much and had been in the trenches many days, so that we were very tired, and thankful to get three or four days' rest in Namur. Then, after that blessed change, we went into the firing again, which was shrapnel, and terrible.

Namur was a very strong place and was not expected to fall; but the Germans had made long preparations for the war, and were bombarding with enormous guns—I saw German guns that took twenty-two horses to draw them.

At Namur we lost a lot of men, because of the heavy gun-fire. All the wounded soldiers and prisoners of war were there; but the Germans did not care about that—they fired on the hospital and smashed it up. When we lost Antwerp the prisoners of war were taken away; but when we lost Belgium we could not keep the prisoners, and the Germans got them back again.

After the battle of Namur the regiment was smashed up, like many others. Every man was looking after himself and trying to find his own regiment, which was not easy.

Here is a photograph of Namur, showing the bridgewhich crosses the river. I was the last man to cross the bridge when we were forced to leave Namur; and for two nights I was in one of these old houses which you can see here in the picture. When I was over the bridge I met a couple of men of my company, and we watched some firing in the distance and felt happy, because we knew that it was the firing of French soldiers, who were just outside Namur.

We were stragglers, and I and a corporal joined the Frenchmen. It was now that many Belgians who were caught by the Germans were shot—yes, in threes and fours Belgians were shot by Germans.

There are good Germans and bad Germans; but more bad Germans than good ones.

We crossed the frontier and got into France, and rested ourselves. I found some of my old friends again, but not all, because a lot had been lost.

In France we made up the regiment again. I had got to Le Havre, and from there I went to Ostende. We had two days in Ostende, then I went back to my dear Antwerp, which was before the Germans got there. From Antwerp I went to Conte, where we had a fortnight's rest, after which we went to Malines. There was not much fighting at Malines, but there had been a lot before we got there, and the place had been destroyed. At that time the Germans were holding the town, but we drove them out. Afterwards we lost it, because they came in heavy numbers, and we could not stop the big guns.

We went up to Conte again about four o'clock in the morning, and later we advanced to Termonde, about twenty-five miles from Antwerp. Our 1st battalion had been ordered to attack Termonde, and the 2nd was stopping outside for reserve.

We saw our 1st battalion go and assault the place; and then we saw it come back, and sad it was to see them, because those who returned were mostly wounded men in ambulances. There were many wounded, as the attack had lasted three hours and our comrades had had to cross the river under fire.

Then it was, when the wounded began to come back in the ambulances, that we were ordered to go in and push the Germans back. We had to go over some fields, and crossing them was like walking on rubber, because of the dead bodies. These bodies had been taken from the trenches, when it was no longer possible to have them there, and had been put in the fields. Sometimes they had been in the trenches three or four days, and we had to eat and drink and sleep with them there. And in the fields that felt like rubber, there were arms and legs and heads sticking out. Ah, yes, it was horrible indeed. And this was the war that the Germans had brought into our little country, which had done them no wrong whatever, and where they had no right to be. It will be the same for them when we get into Germany!

In Termonde it was fierce fighting all the time I was there, and that was for six days. And I tell you that we Belgians did fight; for when we went into Termonde, driving the Germans out, we saw the bodies of women and children and old men that they had massacred—and most of us were crying as we passed them. The Germans can do what they like in wartime, and these were some of the things they liked.

When we saw the Germans at Termonde, after seeing those murdered women and children and old men, we rushed at them with the bayonet, burning to drive our steel into the monsters.

We rushed up to them in our fury, and I drove my long bayonet at a German soldier. I struck at him blindly, but I do not know where I hit him, because at such a time you look after one German and then after another, so that you shall get many of them; but his own bayonet came at me and cut across my right fingers. You can see the scars here—but they are nothing.

It was hard and fierce work; but I was still well. I was tired and sleepy at the end, and was almost killed by bursting shrapnel. Pieces struck me, and one went through my right boot and between the toes. But that also was nothing.

The evening came, and it was just dark. That was October 1st. I had been in the trenches, and was lying down under some trees, resting. Firing was going on still, but we were indifferent to it, and I did not care until I was struck on the right arm by an explosive bullet, a dum-dum. I was lying there, bleeding, with my badly torn arm, for three-quarters of an hour; then some of my friends came and picked me up and gave me a drink and bandaged my arm. At nine o'clock a doctor came along and sent me to a church, which was being used as a hospital. There I spent the night, waiting for the morning, when I was to have an operation.

The morning came, and brought with it one of the strange adventures of a soldier in the war.

I was taken on a wheeled ambulance to a part of the church which was used as an operating-room, and there my torn arm was treated, without pain to me. A nun, who like her other sisters of mercy was a nurse, had the care of me, and she was wheeling me back to my bed.

There was the big entrance to the church near my bed, and as I was being wheeled I saw in that entrance many German soldiers, who were about to rush into the church and seize it.

Quick as thought my nurse wheeled me back, and rushed with me to a door at the back of the church, and out into the open air. She was quite calm, which was well for me, and she hurried me to an English motor ambulance, which was standing at the door and had one English soldier in.

The nun cried to the chauffeur, saying that the Germans were taking the church, and telling him to help her to push me into the ambulance.

The chauffeur, who was an Englishman, quickly and calmly obeyed, and he and the nun got me inside, on my stretcher; then the chauffeur jumped up into his seat, and the motor ambulance tore away and took me into Antwerp. I was in hospital in my native city two days, when the Germans bombarded the city. I was there during the whole of the bombardment; then when the Germans took Antwerp my mother took me out of hospital. There was much excitement and commotion, and it was not a happy thing to be wounded then; but an English ambulance came, and I was asked if I could speak English. I said "Yes."

"Do you want to go to Ostende?" the man asked, and again I said "Yes."

It was a time for haste. A few minutes more, and if I had not been able to speak English I should have been too late, for the train into which I was put by an English marine was the last to leave Antwerp before the Germans entered the city.

Again the Germans came to where I was, and so I had to leave Ostende. I went from there by train to France, and from France I came to England.

I still stop in England. It is a good country, and I feel safe here. It is strange to see beautiful cities not bombarded and smashed by the Germans, and not to see the worst of all—the murdered little children.

If the Germans were in this country it would be just the same, or worse.

I think much of my country, little but beautiful, as it was; but ruined now.

I am young. When I am old Belgium may be as it was before.

I have an eager wish, and to have it fulfilled would make me very happy indeed—and that is to see Belgian, English, and French soldiers march into Germany!

CHAPTER XI

A BLINDED PRISONER OF THE TURKS

[This is a simple, unaffected story of the doings of a young British soldier in Gallipoli and his subsequent experiences as a prisoner of war with the Turks. It is told by Private David Melling, 1/8th Battalion Lancashire Fusiliers. He was a lad when he enlisted, his eyesight was destroyed by a bullet, he was captured on the battlefield by the Turks, and was the first British prisoner of war to be released from Constantinople. The narrator, when seen, was an inmate of the Blinded Soldiers' and Sailors' Hostel, Regent's Park, N.W., the wonderful institution which Mr. C. Arthur Pearson founded and controls with so much success in the interests of those whose affliction he understands so well.]

I enlisted in the Lancashire Fusiliers in November 1914, when I was only seventeen years old, and in June 1915 I went to Gallipoli, where we landed in the night-time. A big ship had been run aground there—the River Clyde—and pontoon bridges had been made at the side of her, connecting with the shore. We left our transport and got into little steam trawlers, which were out at the Dardanelles as mine-sweepers and so on, and these took us to the pontoon bridges. We hurried over them, under fire, and having got ashore we went straight into a bivouac rest-camp. We spent five days in the camp, then we went into the support line of trenches, which is the second line, and after a week or two we went on fatigue.

We were in a Turkish communication-trench, digging it wider, and we came across all sorts of queer things. We dug a dead Turk up, a chap without a head, and near him we dug up one of our short Lee-Enfield rifles. He had equipment on, and when we looked into his pouches we found that he had some of our ammunition, besides his own. We supposed from the look of things that he had been knocked over by a shell and buried in the rubbish. We were throwing the earth out and making the trench deeper when we came across the Turk's head. One chap got it on a shovel and fired it over the top of the parapet. You got used to digging bodies up—it was nothing to strike one with your pick or shovel.

All this experience was good for us, and got us used to fighting before we were actually in it, because there was firing going on all the time, and preparations were being made for charging the Turks with the bayonet.

Things began to get very warm early in August. At about five o'clock on the afternoon of the 6th, which was a Friday, there was a heavy bombardment and a big advance on the left of the Peninsula—that was Suvla Bay. According to the arrangements we were to charge on the Saturday morning, two hours after the bombardment began. The bombardment was to have started at five o'clock; but somehow the Turks got to know about it, and our attack was postponed till ten o'clock. At that hour we were ready for our job.

I shall never forget that Saturday morning at Achi Baba. I had my sight then, and could watch all that was going on. We were on the ledge of our trench, waiting to spring over and rush at the Turks.

Our officer was standing by us, looking at the watch on his wrist—and a terrible strain it must have been.

"Two minutes to go!" he said. And we waited.

"One minute to go!" said the officer next time he spoke.

Then, at ten o'clock, "Over!" he shouted. That's all I remember of what he said. He may have said more, but I can't tell. "Over!" was the order, and over we went.

We all cheered, and then we went helter-skelter for the Turks with the bayonet.

They were said to be two hundred and fifty yards away, but it was a lot more than that—at any rate it seemed so. And the ground we had to rush over was terrible—rough and with a lot of vines about that twined round your feet and tripped you up. Some of our chaps were knocked flat in this way, some fell of exhaustion, and lots were killed or wounded. The best part of our lot were knocked out before we ever got near the Turks.

But when we reached the trench that we were going for we found that there were not many of the Turks left. Our gunners had settled them, so that the trench was full of dead Turks, some of them with their heads blown completely off.

Our task was simple enough. We had to go for one particular trench that was straight in front of us.

I can't give any special particulars about what happened, because it was all a sort of blur, but I remember a few things clearly, and it's these that I am telling of.

The trench was up a hillside, and when I got to it I saw that part of it had been blown up. I rushed at the opening, and fell into the trench. I was alone. I don't know whether I was the first man in the trench or not; but I do know that there were none of our chaps there—only myself and dead bodies.

I scrambled to my feet, and the first thing I noticed near me was a Turkish officer, wounded and unarmed.

There we were, the two of us, the Turk looking at me and me looking at him. I had my bayonet, and I could have settled him or taken him prisoner; but British soldiers don't touch unarmed men, and I was too busy to take him—and a man who is by himself doesn't as a rule make prisoners.

I was looking to see which way to go to get to our other chaps, and the Turkish officer, noticing this, motioned down the trench to the left to show me where they had gone.

I began to clear off to them, but in my eagerness and excitement I did not notice a wire which ran across the top of the parapet. Before I knew what was happening my rifle got fast in the wire at the bayonet-standard—that is, where the bayonet fixes on to the muzzle.

Then an extraordinary thing took place. My rifle was tilted over and the bayonet stuck in the back of a Turk who was huddled up in the bottom of the trench. The first I saw of him was when my bayonet struck him. I looked to see if he was dead, but he never moved. I don't know whether I killed him or not, but if he wasn't dead he was a good actor.

I had been about two minutes—it may have been longer—in getting my rifle clear of the wire, and all that time, for it seemed long, I was alone. When I pulled myself together and went on again in the trench I came face to face with a Turk who was coming from the opposite direction. He seemed to be mad, and made a lunge at me with his bayonet; but it was broken and no good to him. He saw that and turned to run away. As he did so I bayoneted him in the back, and he fell. I could have shot him, but my magazine was empty, for I had been firing a lot.

I passed the Turk and then I found our chaps. It seemed a good distance from where I got into the trench to where I found them—I know I had to go round one or two bends.

When we got together again—and it was a joy to be back with my chums—we were ordered to line the trench. I don't know who gave the order, but it wasn't an officer.

I was the end man of the line, and we were firing hard when a bullet came, and all I knew was that I could not see and that I was lying on the floor of the trench, with one of our chaps bandaging me—I don't know who it was.

I was left there while they went on firing.

I don't know how long I was lying there; but I was terribly thirsty, and drank two bottles of water—my own and one I took from a dead man near me. I could not see him, but I felt by groping about his equipment that he was a British chap.

There were not enough of our men to hold the trench, and they were forced to retire and leave me.

The Turks came up in the trench, and I heard them shouting something like "Garrah! Garrah!" though it may have been "Allah! Allah!"

They were fearfully excited, and I thought it was all up with me then. I never gave myself any hope.

The Turks were running about the trench, looking for our chaps. They ran over me, no doubt thinking I was dead. I was lying on my side, with my hands covering my head, holding the bandages to stop the blood from coming out. I had to do that, because it was only a field-dressing.

I knew then that I had lost my eyes.

I felt as if all the bones in my body were broken with the Turks running over me and stepping on me.

After some time had passed the Turks settled down a bit, not being so excited, and then they began to search the trench and examine the bodies and men in it. Seeing that I was not dead, they propped me up and began searching my pockets. They were talking away, but, of course, I could not understand them. They were not rough just then, but they were afterwards, when I was being led out. They took my pay-book and photographs and everything I had.

I stood up, and then the Turks took me to a communication-trench about ten yards away.

As I was passing them in the firing-line they hit out at me with their hands, trying boxing competitions on me. They dared not have done this if a Turkish officer had been about.

Two more Fusiliers were being led away along with me. They had both been bayoneted, they told me, after they were captured.

I was taken to a place where there were Turkish doctors. One of them gave me a cup of tea. He could speak English, and he asked me how I was. I told him I was pretty bad. I was given a piece of dry bread, but I could not eat it, because my teeth were closed.

It was here that I met a New Zealander or an Australian, a gunner, who had been in the charge. He had no right to be in it, but you could not keep the Anzacs out of the scraps. He said that he and a pal were passing through the place when they saw what was going on. Each of them got hold of a rifle and bayonet and rushed into the charge. The pal was killed and the other man was taken prisoner.

From the doctors' place I was taken to a sort of dug-out, which had some kind of grass in it that felt like heather. The two bayoneted chaps had been taken there as well, and I was very glad to have their company.

I was left in the dug-out all night, with the other two Fusiliers alongside of me. In the morning we were put into oxen carts, four wounded men in each. They were rough things without springs, and were slowly dragged over rough tracks—you could not call them roads—so that it was fair torture to us, bumping all the while.

At last we were stopped at a place and changed into another oxen cart, and taken farther on. We stopped again, and were given a drink out of a bucket—they must have thought we were horses. I suppose they must have been giving a mule a drink, and then it struck them that they might give us a turn. But bucket or no bucket it was a fine drink.

After that I went into a field hospital, and for the first time since I had been wounded I had my eyes properly attended to.

A Turkish doctor who could speak a little English said "Eyes!" then a word that sounded like "yolk." I suppose he meant that my eyes were gone; but I knew that before he did.

After I had been attended to I was put into a field hospital and fed three times a day. First of all we had a ration of bread, which had to last all day, and a drink of tea; about the middle of the day we were given some soup, which the chaps called "bill-posters' paste." It was awful stuff, and the chaps who were badly wounded in the body could not do with it, so they used to tipple their lot into my basin and I would get through it, as well as through my own. I could not eat bread or anything else, because my jaws were affected and my face was badly swollen—it is partly swollen still, but I could just manage to suck the "bill-posters' paste" through my teeth.

It was not until now that I really understood what had happened to me. A bullet had struck me on the left side of the forehead and gone clean through both eyes, just missing the brain, and out at the right side—a wonderful escape from instant death, as our own doctors told me afterwards.

We were given cigarettes in the field hospital—a packet of twenty on every one of the five days we were there; and those cigarettes were a real treat.

At the end of the five days we had another dose of oxen carts, and were jolted in them to the seashore, where we were put into a steamer. They told us in the field hospital that we were bound for Constantinople, and I was rather glad I was going there. I did not want to stop any longer under the everlasting shell fire.

When we went on board we got a loaf of bread and a drink of tea and a drink of water, and that was all we had for the three days we were in the ship. She was full, the place where I was put being crowded with Englishmen, though there was a Turk on a seat above me. I was lying on the floor under it.

It was a great relief to get to the end of the voyage and go ashore. I was taken off the boat, and as we went down the gangway chaps were handing out nice new pieces of bread, hot, and cups of tea. I was lucky, because I had my cup filled twice.

I was taken into a big hall—it seemed to be a sort of drill-hall—and was given another drink of tea and piece of bread. Then we were taken in open carriages, drawn by two horses, to different hospitals. I well remember that my carriage had rubber tyres—and that was very nice indeed after travelling in the oxen carts.

I was carried on a stretcher into a hospital near the quayside, and here I was turned into a sort of Turk, for I was served with a pair of Turkish trousers big enough to fit six of us. They tied round the waist and ankles. I had a shirt also given to me, a sort of big gown which was tied round the waist. We looked like Julius Cæsar in them.

The Turks dressed my eyes and put me into a bed, and I was glad to get in, because I had been thrown about for ten days since I was wounded.

I was in this hospital for about three weeks, treated by Turkish ladies who were acting as nurses. A lady who was there was said to be an Egyptian princess, the late Khedive of Egypt's sister, and she could speak English. She asked me my age, parents' names, occupation and address at home, and said that next day she would write to my mother, to tell her how I was getting on; but when next day came I told her that a chap in my regiment had written home for me. She then told me a bit of joyful news, and that was that I was going to be sent home.

There was a German Bible-reader in the hospital. We called him Charlie, and I will say for him that he was like a brother to us. There are good and bad in every race, and this was one of the good Germans. He brought two Bibles in for chaps to read who could see.

At the end of the three weeks an order came for all prisoners to go into barracks, and I was taken off in a carriage. This time I suppose I looked a real Turk, for I had a fez, though I had my baggy trousers hidden by my khaki trousers, which I had put over them, the Turkish doctor having told me to do this to keep me warm. I scored there, because I don't think that the Turks meant me to walk off with the baggy breeches. But I kept them on all right, and I have them at home now, as a memento.

In these barracks we slept on a long platform, on a sort of thick matting, which was very verminous. At first we were fed pretty well, and then not so well, because the Turkish food is not fit for Englishmen, and they have only two meals a day. They gave us rice and meat, but only a very little piece of meat. The rice was cooked in olive oil, and it seemed good when we were hungry, though we did not care for it. We used to get a ration of bread every afternoon about four o'clock. When that time came our chaps, who were in good spirits, singing and whistling, used to kick up a row and shout, "Hich, Hich!" which was supposed to be Turkish, and meant hurry up with the bread.

It was the Sultan's birthday while we were in barracks, but they did not give us anything extra on that account. The Turkish Christmas was celebrated in August, too, but we never heard anything about it.

The American Ambassador came and visited us and gave us forty piastres each, equal to six and eightpence. The Ambassador used to come round to see that we were well treated, and we were always glad to see him. Through his efforts I got released, and was then sent into the American Hospital in Constantinople. I was there about a week, after which I was put in charge of two American sailors and sent to Dedeagatch, in Bulgaria, the place that has been bombarded lately. We stayed in a place called the Hôtel London, supposed to be the best hotel in the town; but the sailors said it was nothing but an old shack. We were paying for our food and so on, as the Ambassador had supplied us with money for our fares and keep, and the two sailors looked after me all the time.

After two or three days' rest a train journey of a day took us to another town called Drama, which is in Greece; from there we went to Salonica, where 1 was handed over first to the American Consul and then to the British Consul, who passed me on to the military authorities. The British commander-in-chief asked me some questions about officers who were prisoners of war, and so on, and I told him what I could.

For a fortnight after that I was in a hospital ship in the bay, the Grantully Castle, happy and well looked after; then we went to Lemnos and on to Alexandria, where I had another spell in hospital—four days. Then it was really a case of homeward bound, for I was put on board the Ghurka on November 7, and we sailed for Southampton. On board the Ghurka we had concerts and a good time until the 19th, when we reached Southampton. I went to St. Mark's Military Hospital, Chelsea, then came to this wonderful place, St. Dunstan's Hostel, which Mr. C. Arthur Pearson founded, and where I am very happy and learning poultry farming.

CHAPTER XII

HOW THE "FORMIDABLE" WAS LOST

[Just after the New Year, 1915, had broken the British battleship Formidable, successor of the famous ship with which the name of the gallant Rodney is so closely associated, was lost while steering westward in the Channel. In the official announcement it was stated that the cause of her loss was either mine or torpedo, but it was not known which. Later, however, it was stated in the House of Lords that she had been twice torpedoed. The Formidable was a pre-Dreadnought of 15,000 tons and 15,000 horse-power. In herself she was not a serious loss; but she carried a crew of between 700 and 800 men, and of these only 201 were saved. Once more the unconquerable spirit of British seamen was shown, as will be seen from this story of the only survivor of his watch— William Edward Francis, who was a stoker in the lost battleship.]

I had what I take to be a narrow escape of being lost when the three cruisers were torpedoed in the North Sea.

I had been called up from the Royal Naval Reserve and drafted to the Cressy, which, with her sister ships the Hogue and Aboukir, was lost; but almost at the last moment I was transferred, with a chum, to another ship.

I was spared to take a part in the victory of Heligoland Bight; then afterwards, from a port-hole of my own ship, the Formidable, I saw her sister, the Bulwark, blown up, with the loss of nearly every man on board. We were moored close to the Bulwark at the time, and it was a terrible sight to see her go like that. The Germans, however, had nothing to do with the loss of the Bulwark, which was destroyed by one of those mysterious accidents that are bound to happen in a war like this.

Then, on Christmas Day, we had an amusing experience. A German airman came and had a look at things, including ourselves, and he hovered over us, but bolted without even dropping a bomb. No doubt he went back and spun a wonderful yarn of the way in which he had thrown us into a panic, when, as a matter of fact, we only laughed at him.

On the last day of the year 1914 the Formidable was one of the units of a Channel squadron.

She was an old ship, as warships go, but there was a lot of life left in her, especially when bad weather had to be met, and she showed that in the Channel on New Year's morn, for we had run into tremendous seas and a heavy gale of wind was blowing. On the last day of the Old Year the Formidable, like the rest of the British ships, was taking green water on board and she was properly washed. But that was a mere nothing—the British Navy is used to it, and not to hiding in a canal.

That was the way the Old Year went out and the New Year came in—carrying on. It was a stormy ending to a stormy year. Night fell, but there was moonlight, and there was nothing to be heard except the roaring of the wind and the thudding of the seas as the brave old Formidable crashed into them and drove through them, going west.

Go where you will, in any part of the world, you'll find that Englishmen don't let the Old Year die without some sort of feeling and regret, and so it happened that those of us who were not on watch sat in our messes and talked about our homes and those we had left behind us, and of the big things that had taken place in the dying year. The Old Year had truly seen some stormy times, and it was going out in a living gale.

At about twenty minutes past two in the morning I went into the stokehole. The ship was, of course, rolling and pitching and there were plenty of big heaves, but almost as soon as I had got below I felt a heave which I knew could not be caused by any ordinary roll. This heave was immediately followed by a distinct tremble over the whole ship, a shivering which lasted for about ten seconds.

A stoker who had been in one of the bunker-holds ran out and said that water was coming in, and this fact was at once reported to the bridge. It was clear that something very serious had happened, but what it was there was not any means of knowing just then.

Captain Loxley, who was commanding the Formidable, was on the bridge—his little dog was with him—and as soon as he realised what had taken place he did everything he could to try and save his ship and her company. He issued orders calmly and deliberately, and shouted, "Steady, men, steady! There's life in the old ship yet!"

The water-tight bulkhead doors were closed, and a signal was flashed to the other ships of the squadron that the Formidable had been struck; but, as every one knows by this time, orders were given by the Admiralty after the loss of the three cruisers that when a ship has been torpedoed other ships are not to stand by to give assistance. There was reason to believe that the Formidable had been torpedoed, and accordingly the remaining ships were warned to keep off, and they were soon lost to view in the wild night.

After being struck the Formidable became practically motionless, and very soon steam gave out and she was little more than a huge rolling mass on the heaving waters.

At this stage I visited the engine-room and found that the dynamos were just giving out, which meant that the ship would be plunged into darkness, and so add to the difficulty and danger of the situation. But there was nothing like panic on board. Commander Ballard had told everybody to keep cool, and had said that the first thing to do was to get the boats out.

All hands mustered on deck and efforts were at once made to launch the large boats, but owing to the failure of the steam these attempts failed. The ship had been struck on the starboard side, forward, and by three o'clock she was listing heavily and settling by the bows; and it was hard to keep a place on deck.

It was very soon after this that a submarine was discovered near the ship, and I need not say how grieved and furious we were when it was realised that it was impossible to train a single gun on the craft.

After tremendous and extraordinary efforts two boats were lowered and they pulled away into the darkness, crowded.

In the meantime all the tables, chairs and things that would float had been thrown overboard, so that the men who found themselves in the water should have a chance of clutching at something that would help them to keep up, and in addition to this there were the inflated collars which have been provided for the crews of warships since the war began.

Meanwhile the submarine had vanished, but very soon another shock was felt, this time on the port side of the Formidable, so it seemed as if the craft had gone round to make matters even.

"There goes another at us!" some of the men shouted, as an explosion tore the decks and killed a number of the survivors.

"The cowards!" I heard one of my pals growl; "aren't they satisfied at finishing us with one shot?"

It was a natural enough thing to say, but war is war—and British warships are not a canal fleet; they keep the seas and take their chances, and don't slink in hiding.

The lights of a small vessel had been noticed about six hundred yards away, and careful inspection left little doubt that she was a fishing-smack. She did not move and did not make any answer to the appeals for help. Afterwards she slipped away and disappeared, and I'm pretty certain that she covered the movements of the submarine.

Things, however, were not by any means all bad. Four or five miles away more lights were visible, and these came nearer at about four o'clock, when we found that they belonged to a light cruiser.

When the cruiser drew near, Captain Loxley, thinking only of his duty, and wishful that no other ship should share the fate of his own, signalled to her to keep away, saying that the battleship had been struck and that the cruiser might be struck also; but the cruiser swept around the Formidable in wide circles, nobly handled, and showed every sign of being ready to lend assistance.

The effect of the second explosion was to restore the battleship to something like an even keel; but having been torpedoed on each side she naturally sank lower and lower in the water, and it was soon clear that she would founder. Indeed, the first explosion was so terrible that there was little doubt that the ship was doomed, especially in such a sea as was then running. It was perishingly cold, with snow and sleet, and, to make matters worse, a good many of the ship's company were only slightly clad.

Of course there was not the least intention of abandoning the ship until it was perfectly clear that she could not keep afloat, and every effort was made to save her. There was hope that she might be kept going until the day broke, and that then it might be possible to get her into a Channel port; but she had been too badly damaged for such a hope to be realised and she listed terribly.

As the Formidable had been struck on each side water was rushing in very rapidly, through huge gaps, but the ship listed more and more. A fine attempt was made to train the big guns on the beam, and as these represent a very heavy weight, no doubt some good effect would have been brought about, but again there was not the necessary power available, and the effort had to be given up.

Listing more heavily as the moments passed, the battleship at last was almost lying on her side and there was no hope of saving her.

Shortly before this had happened, and when it was known that nothing more could be done, the survivors mustered on the quarter-deck, and it was very strange to see how coolly they accepted the situation—such is discipline and the usage of war, and such is the result of the splendid example which was set for us by our captain and the officers.

The captain remained on the bridge, smoking a cigarette, and some of the men smoked too, while others broke into song.

We had our life-saving collars on, and there we were, waiting for the moment to come when the ship would make her last plunge.

It was at this time that the chaplain, with his hands behind his back, walked up and down the deck, encouraging the men and comforting them—and all the time the most tremendous efforts were being made to launch the boats. This was a task that was both difficult and dangerous, and of four boats that were got out one, a barge, capsized and several men were thrown out and drowned. I might say here that another barge managed to get away with about seventy men, who were picked up by the cruiser, while a pinnace, with a good number of men, reached Lyme Regis, but that was not till more than twenty hours had passed and a score of men had perished through exposure. The fourth boat, a launch, with about seventy men, was knocked about for nearly twelve hours, then they were rescued off Berry Head by the Brixham trawler Provident and taken into Brixham.

But I am getting on a bit too fast—I must return to the quarter-deck of the sinking battleship.

There was near me a little fellow who, a few days before, when the Formidable had sailed, had said good-bye to his mother.

I have six children of my own, and my heart went out to the lad, so I took him by the hand and told him to carry out my instructions.

There was a log of wood floating near, and thinking that this was a favourable opportunity to try and save the youngster, I told him to jump and swim.

The plucky little chap obeyed, but in that heavy sea and the bitter cold he missed his chance, and shortly afterwards he was swept away. It was very pitiful, but there was nothing for it but to take a heavy risk that night.

I saw that there was not long to wait now until the very end came, and so I said to a chum of mine, who was standing near me, "Shall we jump now?"

"I think I'll wait," he said.

I looked around, I saw that there was nothing to be gained by waiting, and so I said, "I'm going. Good-bye," for by this time it was every man for himself.

"Good-bye, Bill," said my chum, and there was a grip of the hand.

Then I dived into the heavy icy sea and made a struggle for it.

The water was bitterly cold, and in a very curious way I suffered intense pain, because the inflated collar prevented me from dipping my head to the breakers and they caught me full on.

Very soon after I reached the water I looked back and saw the Formidable disappearing. She had made a good fight for it, and had kept afloat for a considerable time after being struck by the first torpedo.

When the battleship had vanished the sea was covered with men who were struggling for their lives; but soon the number was lessened, because in that bitter weather only the very strongest could live. One by one men disappeared, numbed and unconscious, while others, like myself, managed to keep afloat and alive.

I was encouraged by the thought that there was a chance of salvation through the cruiser, and I kept on swimming towards her as hard as I could.

For one long dreadful hour I was in that icy sea, battling all the time, until I got up to the cruiser and managed to make them hear my shouts.

Lines were thrown overboard in the hope that survivors like myself could catch hold of them, and I managed to seize one of these and to hang on to it with the energy of despair until I was drawn up near enough to be gripped by some of the cruiser's people—and once they got a grip of us they didn't let go.

I was hauled up on to the cruiser's deck, and a good many of my companions were also rescued by her, so that with the survivors she carried to port and the men who were rescued by the trawler, and in other ways, a round two hundred of the crew of the Formidable were saved. The rest perished.

There is no doubt that the loss of life would have been far greater if it had not been for the skill and bravery of some Brixham fishermen. There happened to be in the Channel that night, not far from the spot where the battleship sank, a little Brixham smack called the Provident, manned by her skipper, William Pillar, and three hands. She was under storm canvas, and was doing her best to seek shelter when the battleship's cutter was seen. The cutter was riding to a sea anchor and was in great peril, while the survivors who were in the little vessel were suffering terribly through exposure.

No sooner did the smack see the cutter than an effort was made to save the men; but in such a sea and at night it was the hardest thing imaginable to undertake a rescue, and it was not until more than two hours had passed and the smack had been handled as only a smacksman can handle such a craft, that a line was made fast between the cutter and the smack and the men were got on board, after a long struggle. They were all transferred to the Provident by about one o'clock in the afternoon of New Year's Day, and they were landed at Brixham, where they were most generously treated, and clothes and drink and food were given to them. At other places on the coast of the Channel other survivors were landed, and very soon we were able to leave for our homes for a little spell of rest.

It is well to remember the very fine life-saving work that was done by fishermen when the Formidable was lost, just as it was done by fishermen in the North Sea when the three cruisers were torpedoed. In their life-saving work at the loss of the Formidable, deep-sea fishermen added one more to the many splendid things they have done for the Navy since the war began.

One result of the failure of the steam was that the wireless could not be worked, so that not much could be done with the sending out of calls; but there was the Morse to fall back on, and so into the night the lamp signals were flashed, warning the other ships of what had happened and telling them to keep clear. They had to obey, having no option in the matter, and it must have been hard for them to leave the old ship to her fate, though I daresay they were comforted by the knowledge that her company were sure to meet their end like good Englishmen.

The Morse signals were understood by the other warships, but it seems that there were one or two other fishing vessels about which would most surely have given help if they had realised what had happened and had understood the nature of the signals. The Provident was packed, having only a very small cabin and her hold and fish-room, but once on board of her the survivors were safe, though as far as room and comfort went, we who were saved by the cruiser were a good deal better off.

I do not want to dwell on the finish of the battleship, and the terrible hour or so I spent in the icy cold of the Channel seas in the very heart of winter. The disaster was so sudden and tremendous that it had a numbing effect on you, and many a poor fellow died through exposure, either in the water or in the boats, which were constantly swept by the freezing seas, so that there was little difference between being in the boats and in the water.

Captain Loxley went down with his ship, you might almost say as a matter of course, his first and last thought being for the safety of his people. Many of the officers went with him, and as for those who were saved, they were all, except one or two who had been ordered to the boats to take charge of them, rescued from the seas into which they had plunged or had been thrown to take their chance just like the men.

CHAPTER XIII

A TROOPER'S TALE

*[It has been said that in this war cavalry have
ceased to exist. As mounted men their opportunities have
undoubtedly been very limited; but in other ways they
have done much to maintain their ancient reputation. In
the earlier days of the fierce attempt of the Germans to
break through the Allied Armies and get to Calais the
teller of this tale—Trooper Notley, of the 5th Dragoon
Guards—was engaged and was finally wounded and
invalided home.]*

There are a good many men who, like myself, were at Mons,
the Marne and the Aisne, and then went into the Fight for the Coast,
and I think they would all tell the same story—that that tremendous
battle was fifty times worse than the Aisne.

The Aisne was very bad; but even there, though the Germans
fought desperately to prevent themselves from being driven back
and turned away from Paris, their efforts were not to be compared
with the determination they showed in their attacks upon the troops
who barred their way to Calais.

The Germans were mad in their resolve to hack their way
through to Paris; but they were madder to break through and get to
the coast, so that they could get within sight of hated England. They
tried all they knew; even as I talk they are trying as hard as ever, but
I'm as sure that they won't succeed as I am that to-morrow will
come.

People have heard and read a lot about the fighting at Ypres
and Messines, and it is of this part of the battle that I am going to
talk, because it was at these places that the 5th Dragoon Guards
shared in a great deal of furious fighting.

We had had a long inning at the Aisne, then our brigade
moved on to the Ypres region, which we reached after being
fourteen days in the saddle. We made a short break at Amiens,
where it was thought that we might have to help the French; but
before long reinforcements arrived for them and we went on our
road to the north, approaching Ypres as the advanced guard of a
brigade.

It had been hard going on the march, and there was plenty of excitement with it, even before we got into the real fight for the coast. There were prowling Uhlans everywhere, and nothing would have pleased us better than to get at them in a thundering charge; but they didn't give us the chance, they are not keen on that sort of thing, and kept in scattered bodies. But at one point quite a little surprise had been prepared for us by about three hundred Uhlans.

We were marching along when we discovered that these Uhlans had taken up a position commanding a road, and they had planted a Maxim, so that they could give us a warm welcome. They soon discovered that we were not going to be caught napping. Instead of keeping to the road we were promptly ordered to leave it and to take to a field running alongside. We made for the Uhlans as fast as we could go, but they did not stop to finish the welcome; they vanished, and I was unable to see the end of them; but it seems that they were completely surrounded and gathered in by some of our infantry.

This was the sort of small affair that was constantly happening, but it was a trifle compared with the real big fighting around Ypres. The cannonade was terrific, and the everlasting firing made it seem as though nothing existed on earth but the thundering of big guns and the screeching and bursting of shells all around.

In and around Ypres, the Allies had pushed far into the enemy's line, and the Germans were concentrating all their men and metal to crumple us up. They strained every nerve and made the most dreadful sacrifices to carry out the Kaiser's command to break through; but though they hurled themselves to certain death, in thousands, they were driven back.

Messines, a village quite near to Ypres, came within the zone of this furious attack, and it was at Messines that most of the brigade, including my own squadron, was posted.

When we got to the village, which we reached by way of the fields—rough going, but safer than the roads—my squadron was ordered to hold the place by the main road, and another squadron went about nine hundred yards up the road and spent the night in digging trenches, which were occupied by the whole regiment on the following morning.

As we moved into the trenches we were under incessant fire, and we were fired on all the time we were in them.

For twelve days and twelve nights we held fast to our trenches, against the onslaughts of forces that were certainly five times as great as our own—and, in spite of their countless losses, the proportion of the Germans was never less than that.

We seemed to have nothing but shell fire and night attacks, and to get anything like decent rest under such conditions was impossible.

There was a curious sameness in this life in the trenches. We had no chance, as we had at the Aisne, of digging ourselves in, because the lie of the land was against us. At the Aisne our positions were very strong and we could afford to smile at the efforts of the Germans to dig us out; but it was a very different matter in country which is as flat as a floor. There was nothing impregnable in our little artificial gullies, and in this absence of help from Nature we had to keep our wits about us to escape the shrapnel and to prevent the nightly visits of our German neighbours.

We were a mixed lot at Messines. Our line consisted of the Connaught Rangers, the Somersets, Bengal Lancers and some Ghurkas—a mere handful compared with the hosts of Germans that were flung against us, with an enormous number of guns. The more troops they sent the more we shot.

Day after day this fighting went on, the German attacks getting fiercer every day. Nightfall was the time when they would make particularly stubborn attempts to drive us out. They would leave their own trenches and advance two or three hundred yards at a time, then throw themselves flat on the ground before beginning the next stage. We had them under observation all the time, but did not let a sound reach them; in fact, we lured them on by seeming not to be there.

On they came, till they were something like fifty yards away, then we got the order for rapid fire, and let drive into the ranks that it was not possible to miss. In this manner great numbers of Germans were destroyed; we punished them terribly, for our rapid fire was certain destruction for their front ranks.

It is not always clear to people, I find, that trenches may be constructed according to the needs of the moment, at all sorts of odd corners and angles. The idea seemed to be that the Germans dug themselves in along a perfectly straight line, while we dug ourselves in along a parallel line a few hundred yards away. In our position by Messines the trenches were splayed out, so to speak, some of them making an angle of ninety degrees or so with each other. We were so entrenched that we were inviting the Germans to step into a hollow square, or rather to form the fourth side of it, which with their heaps of dead and wounded they occasionally did. Of course the positions varied from hour to hour, both in guarding against attempts to enfilade us and in avoiding cross-fire between units of our own forces.

One night a supreme effort was made by the Germans. The Indians had relieved us that very morning, and one troop of our men had got into a barn and cut loopholes in the walls, while another troop had taken up a position at a barricade made up of old wagons and sacks of earth.

At about three o'clock in the morning we suddenly heard the sound of a bugle, and presently the Germans set up a hullabaloo and fairly hurled themselves at our trenches. They came in such strong numbers that the Indians, who had been dealing out death half the night, were overweighted by the enemy, who got round their flank and attacked them in the rear.

A Maxim gun section of the 11th Hussars was hurried down, and from the window of one of the buildings it blazed away at the Germans and covered the retirement of the Indians. The way in which the Maxims have been handled in the war has been a revelation to a lot of people. These handy weapons have been got into upstairs and downstairs rooms and even into the tops of trees, and they have caused terrific havoc in the Germans' solid ranks.

That night affair was desperate; but it seemed as if nothing could stop the mad onrush of the Germans, and at last there was nothing for it but to give way, and so we received orders to evacuate the barn.

Near this particular point the road forks, and a couple of men were left to fire up the right-hand road and two to fire up the road on the left, and for the time being we were effectually covered.

It was at this stage that there arose the chance for a Territorial regiment to come into action for the first time. The Territorials to win this great distinction were the London Scottish.

The Scottish had been ordered up to relieve the pressure, and they came on quickly and in gallant style and took up a position at one end of the barn, while the Highland Light Infantry, the brave old 71st, took up a position at the other, and between them the two carried the barn with a bayonet charge and killed, captured or drove away the Germans.

The Scottish had their baptism of blood in proper good style, with a very strange preparation in the shape of a cunning German trick.

Not far from the Scottish was a windmill which had had three of its sails blown away or destroyed, leaving only the fourth sail, and that looked as if it had been cut clean in half. It was noticed that this crippled sail was working about in the most astonishing fashion, and those who saw it were puzzled to account for the movements; but it was soon discovered that there was a German spy hidden in the mill, and that he was moving the sail to indicate the position of the Scottish, and so bring the German gun-fire to bear on them. When the dodge had been discovered and the signaller settled the Scottish got their own back.

110

By this time I was blazing away from a barricade in an old covered yard, and there was a straggling fire going on all around; but it was clear that we should want reinforcements if we were to hold our own and save Messines.

At last we heard shouts, and I cannot tell you what it meant to us when we knew that the shouts came from our own fellows, and that three battalions of infantry had hurried up and got into action and given the Germans more than they could comfortably carry.

It was at this moment of the saving of Messines that I was struck by a shrapnel bullet and had to leave the fighting-line and come home, with the fight for the coast going on. I had been in it right from the start and had got used to the awful business, even to the "coal-boxes," which the Germans were everlastingly firing. They made a particular target of the church, and for nine days bombarded it before they set the building on fire.

One of the strangest things about a shell is that you never know what it is going to do, and some of the "coal-boxes" acted like freaks.

During this bombardment of the church I watched one of the shells come, and expected that it would do something smashing, for it hit the building full in the middle of one of the main walls. I looked for the wall to be shattered, but the shell never shifted a brick or a bit of mortar; it simply burst in on itself, so to speak, and did no damage to anything except itself, and in the end the Germans got a fire going by sending a much smaller shell, something like a fifteen-pounder.

In a general way of speaking, however, these "coal-boxes" did some terrible mischief when they really exploded, and no living thing within their reach had a chance of escaping. Horses, guns, men, wagons, everything that came within the area of explosions was shattered or wiped out. Often enough men who were killed by the explosions were found in the holes, so that the shell which had destroyed them had also scooped out their grave.

There were all sorts of side issues to the actual fighting. We billeted in every kind of building, some of them very strange; but I think the strangest of all was a cow-house. This does not sound promising; but that cow-house was one of the finest places I ever slept in.

The farm itself was beautiful, and everything about it was on the latest and best scale, so that the cow-house was lighted by electricity, and the fittings were in keeping with the illumination. I had a very comfortable stretch there, and it would not have been possible for us to be better looked after. The proprietor had had notice of our coming and had made every preparation for us, and we were only too grateful for the many good things he freely gave away. We had the same sort of kindness shown to us by the French wherever we came into contact with them.

It may seem somewhat odd that a cavalryman in talking of the war should dwell so much on the trench work and the shell-fire; but in this war a great deal of the work of the cavalry has been dismounted, and practically the same as the infantry, and there has not been the chance that every cavalryman longs for to get to close grips with the enemy's mounted forces.

We had heard so much about the Uhlans that we expected to have some stirring times with them; but these big encounters did not come off, and one great thing we learned about the Uhlans was their skill in avoiding us. We saw them everywhere, but in scattered bodies, and they never gave us a chance of getting at them in the mass. Whenever we formed up in anything like force they melted away; but one fine day we had better luck—we came across them when they were in fair numbers, and before they could perform their vanishing trick we had got at them. At the end we found that we had punished them pretty heavily, for we broke up seven hundred lances which we had captured from them.

CHAPTER XIV

A DIARIST UNDER FIRE

[There is a peculiar interest in any record of experiences which is made while they are being undergone. Imperfect and incomplete though they may be, yet they are of special value because of their reliability. This is particularly the case with some of the diaries which have been kept while the writers were on active service; and extracts from such a one form this story. The author is Private Charles Hills, 2nd Battalion Australian Infantry. His share in the operations he describes was necessarily brief, for he was dangerously wounded, and was partially blinded and invalided to England, prior to returning to Australia. Just before leaving England he was examined by a Medical Board, and it was then found that he was quite blind.]

Lemnos, May 3rd, 1915.

We arrived at Lemnos on the evening of the 1st of May. The place itself is, so far as we can see, just a small island, amongst a lot of other islands, and is evidently a meeting-place for a heterogeneous collection of shipping—cruisers, colliers and cattle-boats. Trading, trawling and touting seem to be the several achievements of this mass. We are lying just inside ... the entrance of the harbour. All night the searchlights play across. Quite a little storm was caused by a small torpedo-boat "arresting" a collier with two shots from her biggest gun. Effective argument it proved. It seems she had not got her sailing papers in order. The defect was remedied.

It pleases the boys to see the neatness and quickness with which the English tars handle their craft, after the slipshod methods of Chinamen and Lascars.

This is just a small island of, roughly speaking, 45,000 inhabitants, solely Greeks. The most outrageous street I ever struck—5d. for a copy of a London daily halfpenny. The least thing seems to be five piastres.

May 4th.

Turned terribly cold last night. Sent us all below to fetch our overcoats. Some of the wounded are telling us terrible tales of maltreatment by Turks of prisoners they take. Evidently we are up against a lot of barbarians. We heard from the front two days ago that the Australians' heavy losses were entirely due to the fact that they charged full speed for a mile and were not content with that, but they must needs go and chase the Turks for five miles. Here they found the position untenable and had to retreat. During this retreat the Turks poured an enfilading fire into them and caused such heavy losses. The Tommy Terriers got just as far and without the enormous loss of life. Some of our fellows who left us at Abbasia suffered amongst the rest: one was killed and several injured more or less. No doubt their example should be to our profit.

May 5th.

We have set sail at last, and every one has gone mad. Of course our destination is unknown. Ammunition is being served out, and extra guards set for torpedo-boats and any hostile craft. The weather is bitterly cold—a vast change from New South Wales. At present steering S.S.W., 6 p.m.

8 a.m., May 6th.

Our move proved to be a very short one, and ended abruptly at about 10 p.m. As soon as we arrived we could hear distinctly the rolling of the guns, and sometimes see the flash of the shells bursting. When morning came we were better able to see where we had got to. The first thing I noticed was the cold. It was "some." The next was the number of boats. Besides our own we counted seventy-six, warships included. On looking round we seemed to be in the Dardanelles itself, but a visit to the map disproved this theory. It seems to me as though we are in the Gulf of Saros, and the narrow spit of land forming the left bank of the Dardanelles was on our right front. Over this, it seemed that the reports were from the guns of warships lying in the Dardanelles itself, bombarding the forts and answering the Turkish artillery in the hills.

We can plainly see the movements of the troops on the hills in front of us with the naked eye, although the distance must be some miles. The air is very clear....

The warships look positively wicked as they glide through the water. There are quite a number of them here. One came up quite close to us this morning. We could see the paint of the guns, no doubt used to disguise them and bewilder any aircraft that may be hovering about over them....

The war is amongst us in real earnest. To-day we have been

treated to what must be one of the most striking sights to imagine. Upwards of a dozen warships have been bombarding the coast-line. It seems as though we were just outside the range of the enemy's guns, and through it being such a bright day we are able to see everything, and to watch the marking of the naval gunners and the effect of their shots. Over fifty transports are above the line of fire, and we are to land under the guns of the battleships. Things are just beginning to get exciting. Long rows of lights are visible. I can only conclude that that is the enemy's rifle-fire.

May 7th.

Well, we have arrived and landed, and contrary to expectations we have marched straight into the trenches. The Turks gave us a great reception, and shelled even the boats we were landing in.

11 p.m., May 8th.

We are now drafted to our respective battalions. Have spent our first day in the trenches. There was quite a gathering of the clans when we joined up, and many old mates were overjoyed to see their friends unhurt. Since morning we have been treated to a consistent dispute of artillery and perpetually shelled with shrapnel and lyddite. The shrapnel is an awfully destructive projectile.

The Turks seem to be filling up their shells with any old rubbish—screws, nails, and even old bolts came in a shell. The worst of it is the occasional sniper in the surrounding bush. He has several scores to his credit. We have one good shot looking for him, and if he only gets a look at him he'll have to close his account quickly. The battalion has been very severely handled, and has lost, roughly speaking, about half its strength. Officers have suffered far heavier in proportion to their men, a brigadier, colonel, two majors and sundry smaller fry have been put out of mess.

I can go no further, as my head is fairly splitting with the noise of shrapnel, lyddite, and the continual lying down doggo in a dug-out.

3 p.m., Sunday.

Unfortunately Turks don't observe the Sabbath, and to-day has been as busy as any other day. To add to my splitting headache last night, I had scarcely any sleep at all for the third night in succession—and the first night in the trenches, with one hour out of three on the look-out. The consequence is a man feels thoroughly washed out. The Turks made one rush against us last night at about 2 a.m., and our boys had all to stand up with fully loaded rifles and bayonets fixed. After a few sharp rounds of rapid fire, however, they thought better of it, and retired and sniped the rest of the night.

The strain of your first watch was more intense than I thought anything could be, and had me fairly mazed for a time. However, I improved and finished up fairly well. This morning, after breakfast, Captain Linklater came along and detailed me for observation work at the right hand of Lewis. Armed with a periscope, I stationed myself at one of the observation-places, and became a target for all the snipers in the Turkish army, I thought. The place was well sandbagged and quite bullet-proof from front and flank, and so I enjoyed a thorough survey of the surrounding country and benefited much thereby....

8 a.m., May 10th.

This morning we have another job in digging a small circular pit ten feet in diameter, to accommodate about four men.... The lieutenant in charge says it is for a guard-room....

Barring a little more confidence and a little more dirt personally the position is unchanged. I am certainly not as nervous as I was at the beginning, although I have not been in a charge yet.

We've had two Indian Mountain Batteries join us, and a great acquisition they are, too. Mule-drawn, they negotiate these hills as easily as the others do the open roads, and they are more accustomed to warfare than the Australian boys are. The Turks won't reply to them at all....

4 p.m., May 11th.

Our position is unchanged, as far as I can make out.... Our much-promised "rest" consisted of navvying a roadway for the artillery, to get one of their big guns up a hill in position....

The weather has been terrible—a real English October day; squally thundershowers and as cold as a March wind, added to which I caught a severe chill last night, and you will see that I am not as happy as I could be. I have no doubt there are some worse off than I, but this is a chronicle of my experiences. Despite the fact that I am wearing heavy khaki flannel tunic, and worsted sweater, and flannel shirt, and another heavy overcoat, I am continually in a shiver. I am anxiously awaiting further symptoms to decide whether it is my old friend pneumonia turned up again. The food (iron rations), corned beef and biscuits and tea, and sometimes a little jam, is not conducive to mirth-producing. In the event of it being pneumonia I suppose it is hospital for me. Several have gone back already with it....

The exploding bullets are largely being used, and in

116

consequence the wounds are much more serious. One of our poor chaps got shot through with one of them, which must have exploded as it reached him. Fifteen pieces of lead were found in his head. Quite dead, of course.

2 p.m., May 12th.

We have spent a quiet morning, after a rotten night. Sent out at 5 p.m. to dig and shape a trench for an artillery pit. We started off all right and presently it began to rain—quite an easy rain, but so wet and cold. We had no blankets with us, and at 10 p.m. there came a halt for sandbags to be fetched. On applying to the artillery officer in charge he considered they were in too dangerous a position to be fetched just then, so we camped in the rain, with no protection other than our overcoats. We waited and waited. No bags came along, and so we slept until four....

This morning we got orders to lie close, as the battery and battleships were going to do a bit of shelling in conjunction. My cold is not changing much, and the cold of last night would not tend to improve matters at all....

We heard a great cheering on the landing-stage this morning. Two battalions of Tommies and the 3rd Brigade, 6000 or so, all told, reinforcing our boys. Probably we shall get more sleep now. I have not washed since last Thursday, six days now not shaven. Some of them have not washed for a fortnight. If you get down to the beach you are under shot and shell the same as anywhere else, so you have a dry rub.

May 13th.

To-day we are back in the trenches in a different space. The Lieutenant-Colonel had us out and inspected us in full equipment. He complimented us on our fine showing, and also told us that the 2nd Brigade had distinguished itself down the coast for this sortie. The news came from him that Sydney had had high holiday over the display of their men. One town, Armidale, the home of Colonel Braund, had collected £365 10s. 6d. for the benefit of the battalion when we arrived at a decent permanent camp. Saw many of the old boys to-day, and looking well at that.

May 14th.

One of our corporals had a remarkable escape from a shrapnel this morning. He and another man were sitting outside the orderly-room awaiting the result of a conference, and they both saw the shell coming. Private Beech moved out of the way, and the corporal turned over and got out of the way just in the nick of time. The shell touched his pants and tore them—another few inches and he would have been blown to pieces....

May 15th.

Quite a quiet night and comparatively still. Had an encouraging sight. About a mile or so away we could see our warships shelling flying troops—and a large body of them, too. Mr. Lowe, our P.C., informed us that it was the main body of the Turks retreating before the allied French, English, and Australian troops. We could see them with the naked eye from one of our shelter-trenches on the hills.

The warships' gunnery was marvellously accurate, and shell after shell fell in the ranks of the enemy. There is a large estimated loss amongst the Turks....

One of the Turkish officers from a neighbouring fort having disagreed with some German superiors, was to have been shot at dawn. In the night he escaped and gave himself up to the Australians here....

The view here is magnificent, but to be appreciated one has to risk one's neck and get up at four o'clock, when things are quiet and only a few snipers about....

May 16th.

The facts and results of the Light Horsemen's charge came out this morning. It seems that somewhere over one hundred went out against the machine-gun on our left front. It seems ridiculous to send out a hundred men on a charge against an enemy well entrenched. Anyway, they got the gun, and lost seventeen killed and sixty or so wounded and missing. It was a victory, as a general result, but costly.

To-day our platoon commander, Lieutenant Lowe, arrived with the telegraphic compliments showered on us by our enthusiastic population. They could not have cheered so hard if they had been as dry as we were.

Water is so scarce that we are allowed only one pint every twenty-four hours. Out of that we have to wash, shave, and provide the means of assuaging a bully-beef thirst. The consequence is I have had about one wash in about two fingers of water since I landed, just ten days ago....

Our sniping friends have suffered severely, one man, a kangaroo shooter, catching four, three of them in half an hour. They fetch him along the line now when they happen to spot one.

The tinstuff is getting monotonous, and I have broken a tooth on those infernal biscuits. Apart from that we have not had much to complain about.

The weather is getting hot in the day and not quite so cool at night, and ever so much more comfortable.

May 18th.

Snakes have made their appearance, though they are small and nervous compared with the Australian specimen. Water is horrible, but, thank God, the weather is cooler, except just at midday, and does not entail a great thirst. Our rations make up for that. Boiled bacon has been added to the menu and is somewhat salt, and that, added to the dryness of our biscuit, and your ration of one pint per day, is — small. In the tucker respect we are much better off than our opponents, who seem to be ill fed, ill clad, and, as usual, ill paid.... The drawback is washing....

May 19th.

Official reports to hand announce that Gallipoli is in ruins, owing to a very severe bombardment from the guns of Lizzie and a few of her ilk. There is absolutely no room for argument about Lizzie being effective. She is a whole army and navy in herself. At the outbreak of hostilities here the authorities were much troubled by the enemy having an armoured train armed with heavy guns, and of course extremely mobile. After it had done much damage Lizzie got her eye on it, and three shots put paid to its account. Their gunnery is little short of marvellous. The boys here are astounded because she puts her shells right over the strip of land we are on, and drops them on some unsuspecting vessel in the Narrows, seven or eight miles away. To get the line of fire and sight it is necessary to use aircraft. We have the great Samson himself here, squinting in the air for us, and are splendidly served in this respect. The Turks gave him a great reception last night, and every piece of gunnery was turned in his direction. Fortunately he was unhurt, being miles off range.

I drew my first issue of tobacco and cigarettes to-day—two packets of cigarettes and 2oz. of tobacco and a box of fifteen matches! Very welcome to a smoker, and I have no doubt they will secure many blessings in the future....

May 20th.

Contrary to expectation the Turks came again, and in large lumps, too. They gave us a perfect fusillade at tea-time last night—rifles, machine-guns, and artillery kept it up till dark. Then we being in the second line of defence (or supports), went to bed. About twelve o'clock Wednesday they started again, accompanied by

119

bombs and machine-guns and rifles. They fairly lighted the night up, and as for row—Bedlam let loose was not in it.

The bombs gave us a bad moment or two. They did not kill any one, but threw up such clouds of dust that we were literally blinded; and then the main attack started at about 2 a.m. on the right and developed all along the row of trenches. A lull occurred till about 3 a.m.

We stood to arms, and then it really began.

First they chanted their war-cry and called on Allah and blew on a little tin trumpet. It sounded terribly weird at that time of the morning—it was pitch dark. We could only stand at our loopholes and strain our eyes to peer into nothingness. Firing continued in a desultory manner. All of a sudden their front wing was in the first line of trenches, which were about eighty yards in front of ours.

Half blinded by the dust and choked by the gas, the boys stuck to it like Britons, and sometimes staved the Turks off. Three Turks did manage to get in B Company's line, but they did not manage to get out again. By this time we had got our bearings, and then the boys settled down to steady firing. Never heard such a noise. I was strained to the utmost pitch of excitement. Times again they managed to get up to the earthworks, but failed to get into the line.

The German officers hooted them on and beat them with their swords; but after the terrible hail of shot one could not be surprised at their jibbing. Two or three officers were shot, with their hard black helmets, proving beyond doubt their nationality....

Last night was a mixture of prayers and curses. Some of the boys yell for Turks to come on—they had some "back at work" shot for them.

The action was continued all day. Casualties were few, owing to excellent cover....

5 a.m., May 21st.

All night long we were waiting for them to come again, but the lesson had been too severe. All day yesterday they sniped and got a few, amongst them our special shot.... I have got the knack of keeping awake all night.

They have landed some 6-inch howitzers from the naval boats, and these are manned by marines. Firing lyddite, and manned by experts, they gave the Turks the time of their lives. The Turkish artillery is outclassed by them. Their big guns on the forts by the shore have a moving platform and consequently were hard to find; however, the boats got wind of where they were, and they started to shell our fellows last night at dusk. The tars saw their flash and fired three shells. Have heard nothing of them since, so suppose they hit something....

Last night passed away uneventfully. Just a little rain of bullets now and then. Also the enemy fired a new kind of shell, believed to be melinite, which stifles a man to death and does not hit one at all. Nice respectable death, after the manner of some deaths!

A rain set in early this morning and brought attendant miseries with it, mud and dampness and general cussedness of every one concerned.

The beggars had the cheek to come over yesterday and demand that we surrendered. After such a pommelling as we gave them two days ago this is colossal. I think they just wanted to spy out a bit more of the defences.

Sunday, May 23rd.

There is a furious bombardment going on out in the harbour. The warships are all standing in close and tackling the last of the main Turkish forts and strongholds in the Dardanelles....

Quite a minor excitement was caused by the arrival of some submarines, supposed to be the pair that slipped by Gibraltar some days ago. The fact that first drew our attention to them was the small or mosquito craft which were running all round in circles, and the bigger vessels were all on the move. Nothing was heard as to whether they were captured or sighted again. I suppose the idea was to keep a good look out and also to provide a much more difficult mark than if they were standing still.

I had a night's sleep last night, the first undisturbed since we landed sixteen days ago. I feel splendid this morning, Sunday—not much like our usual one, though. I absolutely pine for St. John's, Wagga Wagga, for their singing and for one hour of Canon Joe Pike. Tommy Thornber is with me in this respect. The most profitable hours of my life were undoubtedly spent there....

The Turks around us are very quiet to-day. It is Sunday, so they ought to be.

Empire Day, May 24th.

Peculiar thing—the long-expected armistice arrived to-day, instead of yesterday.... I, being of fair size, was one of the assorted few who were to form the burial party. We set out at 8 a.m., and started carting the Turks to their own lines and handing them over to their friends. To attempt to describe the condition of the bodies, some of them having lain out in the sun for twelve or fourteen days, some of them since they landed a month ago, would be futile....

A line of flags was drawn equidistant from both lines, and each party of men kept between their line and the centre line of flags. As this line of flags was made up by one Turk and one Australian alternatively, we had a good view of live Turks. In point of physique they are not our superiors, as I imagined, but of a stock top-heavy—all-chest-and-no-legs sort of build; dark almost to blackness, with such a variety of casts of feature that they cannot be said to possess a distinctive one.

The officers are undoubtedly German—that is, the principal; and a scowling, evil-looking lot they are, though some of them attempted to ingratiate themselves with our boys by offering cigarettes and so on. The body-carting finished about one o'clock, and such work as exchanging ... equipment has been going on.

May 25th.

The submarine that was reported three days ago got in her work on the Triumph this morning at about 12.30, and she sank in seven minutes. The loss has thrown quite a gloom over the trenches here in camp. Our boys could see the survivors struggling in the water and saw the old ship sink, and could not raise a hand to help them in their trouble. As a loss to the Navy it was not a big one, as she was one of the older class of vessel, and from what I can gather we did not lose many of the crew....

I snatched about an hour's sleep this morning, or I should have seen the disaster to the Triumph....

May 26th.

The number of men lost was only fifteen in the sinking of the warship yesterday.... Our socks are stuck to our feet, and the blend of the smell of our socks, chloride of lime, and dead Turks is a subject for a connoisseur....

May 27th.

To-day we have had our welcome spell. Never before did men stretch out to enjoy sleep in such circumstances. Our resting trenches are about half a mile away from the firing-line, and the only danger is from spent bullets, whizzing by too high to hit the trenches, and just beginning to drop as they get to us. After the first line that is easy.

CHAPTER XV

A STRETCHER-BEARER AT LOOS

[Continuing the Allied advance in France, the British forces on September 25th, 1915, captured the western outskirts of Hulloch and the village of Loos, and secured an advantage near Hooge. At the same time the French took Souchez and the rest of the region known as the "Labyrinth," and broke through the German line in Champagne. The fighting at this period was exceptionally severe, and was acknowledged by the bestowal of many honours, amongst them the award of the Distinguished Conduct Medal to Private Harold Edwards, 1st Battalion South Staffordshire Regiment, whose story this is. In the official description of the award to Private Edwards, "for conspicuous bravery and devotion to duty," it was stated that "he gave a fine exhibition of the highest courage and disregard of personal danger."]

It was at a place called Hulloch that we battled it out—but it was Loos, all the same. All my fighting and what I saw of it was done in the Loos district. Our division was at Fromelles, Aubers, Givenchy and Festubert, and a lot of minor events, and I came through these engagements very luckily. Our first battle, however, was Neuve Chapelle, though we did not do any actual fighting there. We were in reserve; but from what I learned later this was worse than the fighting-line, because we seemed to get all the shell fire. It was not till the battle of Loos came along that I was unlucky and got "clicked."

I wanted to be a soldier, and the very day we declared war on Germany I enlisted in the South Staffordshire Regiment, the old 38th. I was trained hard for a few months; but that was easy work, because I had been employed in a Staffordshire forge. Then, before the Christmas of 1914 I was sent to France, and got a spell of trench work until March, when, on the 10th, the British captured Neuve Chapelle.

It is not easy to say what stands out most clearly in my mind of those early operations, because what I chiefly remember is Loos; but I know that we were terribly troubled in the trenches and round about them by rats. These horrible things swarmed—they breed like rabbits, or worse—and they went for anything that was going. They were huge, fierce brutes, and I know of more than one case of a sentry on a lonely post who in the night-time got a bad scare because he thought the Germans were on him, when as a matter of fact it was nothing worse than an enormous rat which was out foraging and made a jump at his face.

More than six months passed between the battle of Neuve Chapelle and the battle of Loos. Of course an ordinary soldier doesn't know much of what is happening, and he doesn't pretend to—he has his own business to mind; but we knew for several days ahead that something was coming off, judging by the amount of stuff that went up. What do I mean by stuff? Well, the shells, principally. They were preparing the way, and were smashing up the whole of the countryside. It was really terrible to see what havoc was done by the German shells at Vermelles—streets were blown to bits, churches and houses were just made into rubbish heaps, and as for men, especially Germans, they didn't count. It isn't easy to make anybody understand what happened; but perhaps the easiest way is to imagine your own house and street and the country near it turned from a smiling, prosperous place into a heap of dreary and desolate ruins.

In that battle of Loos we were thrown up against all the latest and most devilish tricks of German warfare, including gas. There was poison-gas and smoke-gas, terrible artillery, awful rifle-fire, and of course the rifle and bayonet. You seemed to be up against every sort of devilry, including the Germans. I suppose you can't expect anything else from them, being what they are.

We were in reserve trenches on September 24th, and on the night of that same day we went up to the firing-line.

It was a miserable night, with drizzling rain all the time. We started at ten o'clock, creeping and crawling through a long communication trench. We did not finish this advance job till two o'clock next morning, and then we sat in the trench and waited for the dawn to break. It was a solemn business, squatting there in the cold drizzle, talking in low tones, and wondering which of us would go down.

It was a lovely morn that broke, and glad we were to see it. Then, at about a quarter past five, the band began to play. And what a time it was, to be sure! It was a terrible bombardment, with the whole countryside shaking and shivering with the crashing of the guns, and your head felt like bursting with the din.

We had to stand this horrible racket for some time. I don't know how long, but it seemed a fair stretch; then the word came to mount the parapet of the trench. It was a high parapet, and ladders were needed to get over it. There were plenty of ladders to each parapet, and as the order was one man to a ladder, no time was lost in getting out of the trench and on to the open ground over which the advance was made to the German trenches.

As soon as the men who were making the attack got over the parapet, the stretcher-bearers went after them with the stretchers. My chum with my stretcher was Private Pymm.

The men of our battalion had their smoke-helmets on, and they looked like devils. And that was a proper thing to look, for they went straight into a hellish fire—no other word will describe the storm of shells and bullets that met them. It seemed impossible for any one to live in it, yet our men went forward, and being a stretcher-bearer I had a wonderful view of them.

As soon as we got over the parapet the men began to fall, and we began to bandage them up. What we had to deal with were mostly "blighty" wounds, as we called them—just one through the thigh, or a flesh wound. We did the best we could for them; and we had soon tackled a few. Then we went on and tackled a few more. We had dropped our stretcher and were hurrying about, each of us doing the best he could.

I had got about ten yards ahead of Pymm, when I heard him shout; but there was such a terrible commotion that I could not make out what he said. We were at that time on the open ground, and it was bad to hear the cries of the poor fellows who were shouting for stretcher-bearers. I was that busy I forgot about Pymm, and supposed that he, like myself, was dressing and bandaging.

People at home in England, with things going ono pretty much as usual in spite of the war, don't realise what cries for help from the wounded mean; but they are very terrible and pitiful, and I shall never forget them. But there is one fine thing about it—you never think of yourself, and the idea of danger doesn't bother you, especially when you're in the thick of it.

At this time the attack on the German trenches was very fierce, and there was a tremendous fire which seemed to sweep everything and everywhere. There did not seem to be a chance of escaping, and sure enough I got caught. I was hit, and I felt it; but I did not know how I was wounded, and I didn't care about it—I was too full of what was happening. And the wounded were crying for help; so I carried on.

I let myself gaze at the sights in front of me. I don't suppose that I gazed for more than a few seconds; but a lot took place in that short space of time, especially where I was.

I was not more than forty or fifty yards away from some barbed wire entanglements in front of me. These had not been properly cleared away, so it meant that our chaps had to rush them as best they could on their way to the German trenches. The wire-cutters dashed up and cut away at the stuff, and the other chaps rushed on with the bayonet. This seemed to me to go on for just a few seconds; but I may be wrong. At any rate, even in that short time, a terrible lot of chaps went down. I did not notice what the wire-cutters really did; but they must have used their wire-cutters well. At any rate, our chaps got through and made the Germans run.

Well, I watched all this for a bit, then I heardo the cries again, and all I thought about then was to try and do something for the poor chaps who were wounded and were so much worse off than I was.

One of our men had gone down, and I hurried up to him and dressed and bandaged him as best I could. He ought to have gone to the dressing-station, but instead of that he rejoined his regiment and kept in the fighting-line for four days more; then, as he wasn't fit to do any active duty, he was sent away. I learned afterwards that this was Company-Sergeant-Major L. Ford, of my battalion, who has got the D.C.M.

While I was busy on this job, several men offered to help me and to attend to my own wound; but I told them that I could manage all right, and wasn't in need of doctoring.

I was in full view of the Germans, but I didn't bother my head about that. I saw, lying in the open, a soldier who was wounded and wanted help, and I started off for him. I walked—I don't remember that I dodged or ducked much, because I wasn't caring. I remember that one of my officers shouted to me to hurry up and get out of it and seek some sort of cover. I shouted back that I was all right and that I didn't mind it. The funny thing is, that officers were so anxious about their men, and never seemed to give a thought to themselves.

I never reached the wounded man, for as I was staggering across the open towards him—I was beginning to feel the effects of my wound—I felt a sharp pain somewhere, and I gradually sank down to the ground and lay there. I did not know at the time what sort of a wound it was, or where; but I knew that it was a bullet, and that I had got a second good 'un which had nearly put me to sleep.

A black cloud seemed to come over me and I went into sweet slumber. I must have slept a long time, for when I awoke I could see only a few soldiers knocking about; but I could hear them still fighting it out. I can't tell what exactly took place behind the mine which was called Tower Bridge or at the quarries, because I was wounded before I reached the German line. What I am talking about relates to the things that happened on the open ground around me when I was wounded, and what I saw in my own neighbourhood at other times. You can't do more than that.

I had a few hours' sleep; then two soldiers came along and I awoke. I asked them to stick me up on my props and give me a lift; but they were wounded, too. However, they did the best they could, and put me up, and I staggered about six yards. Then I fell again, and I remember no more until I heard a fellow shouting, "Here's Edwards, sergeant!" Then somebody said, "Yes—and poor Pymm's lower down here." They were our own stretcher-bearers.

Then, for the first time, I knew that Pymm had fallen. He had gone down, mortally wounded, when I heard him shout. When I learned this it was well on into the afternoon, eight or ten hours after the fight began; and all that time I had had nothing to drink.

There were plenty of the trench ladders lying about, and one of these was got, and I was put on it by my chums and carried to a trench at the back, to the medical officer. Water was either not obtainable or they would not give it to me—I dare say that was it, because later I had empyema—so the medical officer gave me an acid drop; and I made the best of it.

When I reached the trench it started to rain, and I got soaked, for the soil was chalk stuff and the water could not get through. So I had to lie in the water for some hours, and it was not until next morning that I got to the first-aid dressing-station. I was two days more before I got down to the Canadian Hospital, where, afterwards, the medical officer, Captain Parnis, who had been kindness itself to me, told me that I had been recommended for the D.C.M.

By this time I knew that I had been shot through the lungs, and that the wound was dangerous. It was a very narrow squeak; but a miss is as good as a mile, though in my case it meant a long spell in hospital. But everything that it was possible to do for us was done, and outside people also are very kind; they write to you and come and see you, and they send you things—sometimes tracts, which you don't want. My picture was given in the papers and kind things were written about me, and the idea got about that I was a mere youngster. I dare say that was the reason why some children sent me a Christmas-box—thinking, perhaps, that I was their own age. They sent me half a dozen cigars—realo cigars; a little wooden horse, and a "platter" dog, as we call that sort of crockery in Staffordshire, filled with chocolates. I valued the children's gift all the more because I am young—just out of my teens; I was in them when I enlisted—so I have a lot in my favour, and hope soon to be quite well again.

Here's a letter from one of the officers of my regiment—he

wrote to my dad, too—saying how proud they are because I've got the D.C.M.

Well, I do feel proud, too, naturally; but it came as a great surprise to me, for never did I think of such a thing; and when people speak to me about it, I simply say, "I only did my duty, as others have done."

CHAPTER XVI

A FUSILIER IN FRANCE

[The following story of a baptism of fire and subsequent experiences at Loos and in France is told by Private Fred. Knott, who, soon after the war broke out, left civil life at the call of duty and enlisted in the Royal Fusiliers. Like so many present-day soldiers Private Knott kept a record, under fire, of many of his experiences, until he was wounded and invalided home. From this selection we become more intimately acquainted with the life of our men not only in the trenches but also, which is equally interesting, with their doings when they are resting and able to share in the foreign life around them. We have had abundant proof during the war of the considerable powers of observation and description which so many of our fighting men possess.]

A year's hard training had got us more or less used to marching; yet when we got to Bethune we were nearly all done up, for we had been on the road three days. We eagerly sought our billets, which in my own case happened to be an attic in an empty house. Our "cookers" followed us, so that next morning we had a good breakfast; then we raided the pump at the back of the house, hurried through a wash and sallied into the street, where we saw a sight that will not be forgotten.

There was an almost continuous procession of ambulances, full of wounded men from the Loos front; and an endless stream of men of all regiments were walking down the street to the dressing-station. The British soldier has a happy knack of looking at the bright side of a gloomy picture, and even now amusement was caused by the spectacle of one or two Scotsmen wearing Prussian Guards' helmets and walking along quite unconcerned about their wounds, most of which were in the arm.

In the afternoon we left our billet for the trenches. At the first halt a party of 200 German prisoners passed us. I have never seen such a collection of dejected, worn-out individuals. One man, who was apparently a non-commissioned officer, leaned on the arm of one of the guards for support, and his face was the picture of despair and misery.

Knowing what this war means to France especially, and what the French have had to endure from Germany for over forty years, it was very interesting to notice the attitude of quite little French children towards the captives. These boys and girls, standing on the pavement, insulted and spat upon the Germans, who, however, took little notice of them.

On the road we passed some of our own Tommies, coming from the trenches, and rejoicing in their relief. They wanted to cheer us, and shouted, "Hurry up, chaps; there's plenty left for you to do up there." They were quite right, as we soon discovered.

From Bethune we marched to the town of Vermelles, where we had our first glimpse of the havoc caused by the enemy's artillery fire. The whole place was a mass of ruins, very few houses remaining intact. What had been a town had been smashed by German guns to a vast mass of rubbish. It was a melancholy sight, yet it strengthened the determination to do our best to overcome the tyrants who had brought about such widespread misery and ruin. To make the sight all the more impressive, we distinctly heard the booming of the guns as we marched along.

Another sight which filled us with silent reverence was a graveyard on one side of the road—graveyards, big and little, have sprung up in all sorts of unexpected places on and near the battlefields. There were many simple wooden crosses marking the graves of British soldiers who had fallen earlier in the war. The sight of these resting-places took the mind back to those terrible days when our men fought so magnificently against almost hopeless odds, and solemn thoughts came, almost unbidden, to many of us as we went on marching towards the trenches to get our baptism of fire.

Outside the town another halt was made to let some cavalry pass. We had to wait at least a quarter of an hour for this—and a fine sight it was to watch the passing of these mounted men, for the nature of this war has made it quite a rare thing to see considerable bodies of cavalry.

After leaving the main road and taking one or two cross-cuttings we found ourselves in a wild, desolate field, covered with fairly large shrubs and weeds. It was one of the most miserable and depressing fields imaginable, and to crown its wretchedness rain was falling heavily and steadily and the ground was sodden.

The ammunition mules were in the rear, and we were served out with 130 rounds each. This looked like real business, and when it was over we extended in artillery formation, and cautiously advanced along the field. Everything now was done as if we were actually in the presence of the enemy, and there was a singular thrill and excitement amongst us and a constant wonder of "What next?"

We had moved a considerable distance, when we reached a reserve trench. We were ordered to enter it, for obviously it would have been fatal to go any farther by daylight.

In this trench we were concealed until it was dark. We were in great discomfort owing to the rain, and we were almost knee-deep in mud. We were not sorry when, as evening fell, we got out of the trench and again advanced in artillery formation; but only for a few yards.

The order was now given to lie down, for the enemy flares were going up one after the other, and it seemed as if at any moment our presence would be made known and a heavy fire directed on us.

The long marching and exposure to the bad weather had had their effect upon us. We were sodden, and in addition to the weight of our clothing and equipment and ammunition we had the weight of the rain and the mud, so you can easily understand that as we lay flat on the ground we dropped off into a heavy sleep.

I don't know how long we slept—I don't think it was long—but we were galvanised into wakefulness in a second, for a shell had burst not more than twenty yards in front of us with a terrific report, and a shower of earth fell on us.

That was the beginning of my baptism of fire, and it was the most startling awakening I ever had. It was a stern warning, too, and we quickly retired to another reserve trench a short distance away and jumped pell-mell into it. There were some good goers that night, in spite of heavy ground and heavier equipment; but we soon recovered our composure when we were in the trench, and laughed and made the best of it.

From this reserve trench we entered the main communication trench, and here we had one of those mysterious and unnerving experiences which have been so often known in this tremendous war. Progress at the best was slow and difficult, but it was made far worse because of the repeated issue of the order, "Retire!"

For some time we kept going "about turn," up and down the trench, though when word was passed down the line all our officers denied having made use of the term, and they urged us forward.

This strange matter gave us something to talk about for a long time, and the general feeling was that it was the work of a German spy, though the mysterious agent was never discovered.

We were now getting really into the thick of things, and two companies of the battalion made their way into the firing-line, while my own company went into reserve; and there we had our first touch of gas, though luckily without any serious loss of life. When the gas attack had passed we tried to snatch some sleep, but this was impossible, as we were quickly detailed for various duties, such as ration-carrying and supplying the first line with ammunition. I found myself at the latter task, and started out to find a regiment which was holding the front line on the right.

And now I had one of those awful experiences which have so often fallen to soldiers in this war—one of the things which, little in themselves, mean so much to the individual, especially to one who has not got accustomed to such warfare as this.

After making my way through countless trenches, some of which were empty and absolutely reeked of gas, I found myself in a narrow ditch—it could not be called a trench—which was literally filled with dead bodies. Snipers' bullets were whizzing all around me, and often I had to take cover by lying alongside a dead comrade. Each side of the ditch was strewn with bodies, the wounds on which were too ghastly to be described. Thoroughly sickened at the sight, I had to press on, treading on poor fellows' bodies all the time. It was truly horrible, but the ammunition had to be got there, and this was the only way to get along.

At last I reached the regiment I wanted, and found that it was keeping up rapid rifle fire. Leaving the ammunition with an officer, I started on my homeward journey, which I thankfully accomplished, but with great difficulty. I was very much impressed by the flares as I went along, and I do not exaggerate at all when I say that they were distinctly reminiscent of a firework display.

Reaching my own lines, I found that I was not wanted for any more fatigues, so I thankfully crept into a dug-out at the rear and fell fast asleep.

Early next morning we attacked the enemy, and I got my proper baptism of fire. Two of our companies had gone into action and had lost rather heavily, and my company was ordered to reinforce.

I was amongst the men who were chosen to reinforce, and leaving the reserve trench we passed into the fire trench and so over the top, amid a shower of bullets.

The Germans were hidden in a coal-mine near the famous "Tower Bridge," and it seemed hopeless to try and dislodge them; but the British had determined to have a try, and so we advanced, dropping now and again for cover. Here again the ground was strewn with bodies, and often it was necessary to use one of them as a covering screen.

It became necessary for some of us, myself amongst them, to withdraw to the original fire trench, and there we remained for two days. On the second day a lull in the fighting occurred, though there was a sharp watch on both sides and rounds were exchanged. A strange thing happened at this stage of the fighting. One of our N.C.O.s, going through a deserted fire-bay, found a man in khaki who was behaving in a very mysterious way. The N.C.O. grew suspicious, and with the help of two privates he marched the man before the colonel. The man said he was a Welsh Fusilier, but one of our men who had previously served in the Welsh Fusiliers soon showed that the statement was utterly false.

The man was searched, and then the amazing discovery was made that he had no fewer than a dozen identification-discs of different regiments.

Further questionings showed beyond all doubt that he was a very bold and cunning spy, and he was shot with very little ceremony.

Another day passed, and at night we were relieved. When we marched back through Vermelles we were utterly exhausted, and I dare say we looked pitiful objects, for we were thickly covered with clay and were minus the best part of our equipment; but we were proud, all the same, and I think the pride was justified, for it must be remembered that many of the men who took part in the very heavy fighting at Loos were soldiers who, like myself, had only just had their baptism of fire. They had at any rate done their best to uphold the tradition of British courage and endurance.

Trench life forms such an immense feature of the war that it will be interesting, I dare say, to give a little detailed account of it, just to show how closely resembling animal and savage conditions are those which have to be endured, and which, as a rule, are borne cheerfully and in a thorough make-the-best-of-it spirit.

We had been ordered to go to the trenches, this time on a new front. The line was situated on a canal bank, and we took up our position at night, carefully picking our way, helped by the lights of the flares.

At the end of our journey we found a series of dug-outs at the side of the water, and I and my chum quickly claimed one of them. This dug-out just conveniently held two men, though space was very limited. The prospect was not promising, but two heads were better than one, especially on active service, and soon we had rigged up the "mac." sheet and the overcoats and made a cosy bed, and we made ourselves comfortable. We were the better able to do this because the night was mild and the firing confined to an occasional shell—a mere nothing as a disturber of harmony. The next order was a cup of café au lait, and I don't think people at home realise what a joy it is to set to work on such a little treat as this.

My chum carried a small, compact spirit-lamp, and with this and a tin mug we soon had a glorious steaming drink ready. We dwelt on it as much and as long as we could, then settled down to sleep, making ourselves snug by covering the doorway of the dug-out with a piece of old sacking. This was1 not an easy matter, for the enemy had become aggressive, and a heavy bombardment started. It was bad enough to make us open our doorway and look out, and we soon saw that the shells were finding their mark in the canal in front of us, sending the water up in great sprays. This we could easily make out by means of the brilliant flares. Now and again a shell missed fire, and we just saw it as it plumped into the water.

Higher up in the officers' dug-out a gramophone was playing, and amid the sound of bursting shells we heard snatches of songs that carried our minds back to England and home. Later the shelling ceased, and once more we tried to sleep. This time a new trouble arose, in the shape of huge rats crawling over us. By means of candle-light we started destroying them with a bayonet; but this was a difficult task, for the rats often enough were swifter than the jabs at them. There were plenty of squeals in the dug-out, and these and our own cries mingled with the shrieks that came from rats outside, both in front and rear of the trenches, which were fighting pitched battles. This uncanny and unpleasant hunt in the dug-out ended in time, and we managed to gain a little rest. I am reminded that in one lot of trenches which we occupied in another part of the line a tree-trunk had fallen across the fire-bay, and at night a continual procession of rats could be seen crossing it, in spite of repeated slashes at them with bayonets.

Next day we had an opportunity of scanning the surrounding district. Farther along we could see the damaged steeple of a church, once a handsome building, now in ruins, for it had proved a good target for the German guns. On the opposite side of the canal several fine trees had been struck down, leaving blanks in a stately avenue. I gazed at the canal itself and wondered how many brave fellows' bodies had found their last resting-place there, for it was the scene of a big advance earlier in the year. But my reflections were cut short by military duties, and I was detailed for various tasks, such as rifle-cleaning, fetching rations, etc., while my companion made a fire to cook the breakfast. We now settled down to a more or less regular routine, and waited our turn to strike an offensive blow at the enemy at the first opportunity.

It is usual after a spell in the trenches for a regiment to retire to a village in rear of the firing-line for a rest, and I was always glad of this change, because it afforded many a strange sight to me, an average British soldier. We reached our village at about four o'clock in the afternoon, and each platoon found itself billeted in a barn at one of the farms which abounded in that particular locality. Here the town-bred man had the chance to study foreign rural life, a little hobby which helped him for the time to forget the trenches and their inevitable discomforts and dangers.

After a time we easily adapted ourselves to the rough straw beds that were provided for us, and we very soon found that we must not object if we had a ferret or two in a cage quite close to the bed. As a matter of fact we were soon on good terms with the fierce little creatures, which have proved splendid friends to the soldiers in the trenches in hunting and killing the swarming rats.

When we went out on voyages of discovery we found that the typical village contained one or two estaminets—they are rarely called cafés in the rural parts of France—and possibly one or two little shops—épiceries—which sell a variety of things appealing to a soldier's simple tastes. At certain hours the British Tommy is allowed in the estaminets, where such drinks as beer and red and white wines and the customary café au lait are obtainable cheaply. It is found from experience that these places rarely have change for paper money, which at times is rather awkward, especially when combined with a vague knowledge of the language; and the usual reply is "No money"—truly a poor consolation to a thirsty soldier. In time, however, we became known to the keeper of the estaminet, and when money became circulated the difficulty was remedied. A brief stay in a village was enough to make the villagers friendly, and little kindnesses on both sides became a common practice.

A characteristic of every place was the lack of facilities to obtain extra meals, though at certain estaminets a good repast of fried eggs and chips, with an occasional dish of stewed rabbit, was procurable.

This is merely a glimpse of the peaceful and gladly welcomed break in the life of the soldier who is on active service. It makes you all the more fit for the trenches and that night sentry duty to which you are so often roused in your dug-out by the corporal shouting, "Next relief!"

CHAPTER XVII

THE DAILY ROUND

[By way of contrast with the diary which was kept in Gallipoli by an Australian soldier, and is given on page 180, and as an admirable companion to that work, there is this diary of a young officer, kept by him while serving on the Western Front. The diary is of the small, leather-bound pocket variety, and it was kept by means of the little pocket-pencil accompanying it, in small, yet clear and coherent writing, despite shell fire, bombs and other warlike elements. The extracts are made exactly as they were entered from day to day, and they form a deeply interesting record of what is "the daily round, the common task" of a very large number of junior officers who have undergone precisely the same experiences with unfailing cheerfulness and courage. The writer after serving in an Officers' Training Corps, was posted to a Service battalion of a famous old Line regiment.]

Dec. 13th, 1915.

Marched to —, seven miles. Water in places up to the knees. No billets for B Co. on arrival.

Dec. 14th.

Marched to —, three miles.

Dec. 15th.

Marched up to trenches, —, eight miles. Awful condition. Big craters in front, and three saps in our line.

Dec. 16th.

Narrowest escape of self yet recorded. Shell burst in trench and killed man one and a half yards away and blew your humble into the mud, together with another C.O. and others. Two other men wounded. Felt a bit shaky for some time.

Dec. 17th.

Relieved for forty-eight hours and marched to —, four miles. Good billets. Delicious shave and wash, and two glorious nights in my valise.

Pass into —, to see H. No luck—on leave. He returned ten minutes after I left for —.

H. ran over to see me, and we had two full hours' "jawing," and café au lait. Left for same trenches at 12.30. Had a warm reception with artillery, and owing to some "show" in the vicinity had to stand-to for hours. Raining hard and mud knee-deep—miserable, and thought and thought of the happy home, and wondered and wondered! Went out on patrol with one man at five next morning, but had to return post-haste, as three of the enemy were on similar job and washed our intentions out.

Shelling all day, both sides. Few men hit.

At stand-to, 6 a.m. Much shelling. Very uncomfortable. At 7.30 an enemy mine went up—a fearsome thing. The sensations were these—

I. A horrible rocking of the trench.

II. A tremendous dull roar.

III. A huge column of earth rising higher and higher into the sky.

Then came the falling matter, we lying in the bottom of the trench, while everything imaginable fell around—earth—huge clods—sandbags and timber. One big piece of wood landed with a thud a foot from my head and spattered me with mud. Escape No. 2 since I joined. Fortunately the mine was lifted just beyond our saps, and presumably in the same place as the crater. No one was seriously hurt—only two slightly knocked about. Of course an attack was expected, but none came, and we stood-to till 8.30. Had an awful time from mine explosion till we were relieved at 2.30 p.m. Marvellous how we all escaped. I thought my number was up every minute, and my nerves were not of the best and I was feeling a bit rocky. While relief was being carried on we had an awful time: all kinds of shells, big and small, landing everywhere. Very fortunate to get out with no casualties. Incoming regiment had a few. At 11.15 p.m. I returned to trenches in order to go out again on patrol. Was out for thirty minutes, took survey and returned safely, covered with mud and pretty wet. Returned to — Farm, where my platoon is billeted. It is a small fortress, built up with sandbags from a big ruined brewery. Last night while asleep, about 3.30 a.m., a big shell burst just outside my cellar door, and again I thought my number was up. Earth, etc., was shot into my abode, and the doorway blocked up, not to mention bricks; but I was left intact.

Shelling this ruined village — all the morning, and the trips to the men at meal-times were very risky, the latter being in another keep 150 yards up the road. One had to dash for it every time. Shelling remained hot, so had to remain at the mess till after tea, 4.30 p.m.

Gas attack from our trenches at 9 p.m. Quiet for ten minutes, then fearful shindy. Stood-to in our redoubt, but had to get to cellars when shelling started—and such shelling: the worst I've ever experienced. They came in dozens. Then we began, and the noise was hellish. They fell all around us and some hit the shattered walls, making a hail of bricks.

I felt a peculiar tightening round the heart when one of the big variety buried itself under the cellar wall I was in and failed to go off. It fairly seemed to lift the floor, and the sickening thud was as bad as the fearful racking explosions. It was nothing short of miraculous that our cellar got off scot-free.

All this time we could see through our loop-hole the explosions of the shells on the trenches, 300 yards to the front, and by their light and the light of the German searchlights and fires we could see the huge clouds of gas on their death-dealing errand.

The Germans put huge fires on their parapets to lift the gas over their heads.

It was an unforgettable scene, with their and our own star-lights making night into day. It was indescribable pandemonium.

The shelling died down after a couple of hours, and we stood down and tried to sleep; but it started again at 12.45 a.m. for an hour, and again at 4.45 a.m.; and this practically meant stand-to all night.

One of the worst nights I've spent out here—in fact, the worst.

About 2 a.m. I got word that —, one of our B Co. officers, was killed while waiting to go out on patrol to ascertain the effects of gas on enemy. He was a fine chap, and most popular, and even now it is difficult to believe he is really gone. Another lucky escape for us (B Co.) that we were not occupying the trenches. They were blown out of all recognition and the casualties were awful, the lines being strewn with dead and wounded and buried men.

The trench occupied the previous night by my platoon is absolutely gone, and only six men are left in the platoon holding it at the time of the "show."

Shelling continued all the morning—most uncomfortable, and we had many narrow escapes, walls round us being blown to h—; but still our cellar got off. We were relieved at 12.30, and, things being quieter, we got off down the road at top speed.

What joy to see actually motor buses waiting for us three miles back, which took us by way of — to —, a small village where our few days' rest and incidentally Christmas, will be spent. The change will be much appreciated by yours truly. I have just had my first wash and shave for four days, and feel cleaner than ever before in my life; and in a clean change and new suit I wouldn't call the King my aunt!

A delicious surprise was the sight of H. on the road, waiting for me as our convoy of buses neared——. We had a good chat, and I hope to see him to-morrow again.

Morning with platoon, cleaning up, etc. Afternoon obtained pass to go and see H. Had a glorious Christmas Eve, far beyond expectations. Good tea, theatre, dinner, and two hours' solo. Fine evening. Came back on the carrier at 10.30.

Christmas Day in France.

Up at 6.30 and marched bathing party into —. Left them and looked up H. In bed; got him up and had breakfast with him and a walk round, and marched my party back here — by 10.30. Wrote two letters and found five waiting for me—long-delayed ones. This was a fine Christmas gift.

11 a.m. Went over to men's sports till 12.30 lunch. Helped to pay out from 2.30 p.m. till four. Tea and chat till dinner; chicken and plum pudding. Very good. Talked till 10.30 and then to bed. Very quiet evening, during which my thoughts were for the most part with the dear old folks at home....

NEXT CHRISTMAS???

Quiet day. Morning, church parade and men cleaned up. Afternoon, other officers out, so I was O.C. for the time being. Spent two hours censoring eighty letters! Quiet evening. Dinner and chat; bed 10 p.m.

Heavy bombardment going on in distance.

Morning, getting ready to move.

Moved at 2 p.m. Raining.

Got into trenches at 4.30 p.m. In reserve, 1500 yards from enemy—and a nice change for B Co.

At night I went on patrol with a man to find a way across country to A Co., who were holding a line to our right front. Awful going, but got there. Came back by road through — village and Danger Corner. Out two and a half hours.

Slept as well as I could on a narrow board till 7.30 next morning.

Quiet day. Went out at night with C.O. Got lost, and were out three hours. Good joke.

Quiet day. Went out in the morning on voyage of discovery round old trenches. Went in to the left shoulder in mud and water. Another good joke!

Quiet day. A few shells on the right; but we were left alone. At 5 p.m. I went out with a party of seventy, carrying all kinds of things to the front line. Out till 8 p.m. Quiet night.

A wet day. The road behind was shelled heavily all day, but fortunately it was quiet while we were being relieved after dusk. Had the real Bank Holiday feeling on getting to reserve line billets two miles away, and enjoyed a splendid night in my valise. Had onedrop of whisky at 9.30 p.m. to drink the health of the New Year; but sleep was by far the most important thing, so to bed at 10 p.m., to dream of home and the dear old past.

Woke during the night to hear the guns in the back garden booming in the New Year, and shaking and rattling walls and windows. Dreams shattered!

What luck for the New Year?

How fervent is the hope for a glimpse of the end before many of the new months have gone.

In the morning looked round the men and inspected several

things, followed by a little revolver practice. Had a sleep, or tried to, after lunch; but attempt was futile, owing to thoughts.

Went out with party of fifty at 5 p.m. to the trenches, repairing roads, filling up shell-holes, etc. Returned at 9 p.m., and to bed.

Sunday, Jan. 2nd.

Church parade in top floor of rickety old barn at 11 a.m., followed by an impromptu Communion Service, during which my thoughts wandered.... These services always touch me more than anything else I know of, and unbidden thoughts rise and fill me with longings and yearnings that are inclined to be unpatriotic, as well as bringing the familiar lump to the throat which every one experiences out here at times, and a queer feeling round the heart.

Afternoon, went to — in company with other officers in motor lorry, to attend lecture on telescopic sights and sniping. Returned at 6 p.m.,and joyfully found I had just missed a working party to the trenches.

Tucked myself in my valise at 9.30.

Jan. 3rd.

Platoons cleaning up. Inspected rifles, etc. Had my first lesson in riding. Felt rather insecure at first, but found the "bump" after an uncomfortable 100 yards jogging about, to the great delight and amusement of my men; at which I joined in. Had a small gallop before finish, and stuck on.

Afternoon, writing letters and reading, and out with working party to the trenches at 4.30 p.m., mending shell-holes in roads, etc. Returned at 9 p.m., and to bed.

Jan. 4th.

Relieved and went to — for a four days' rest, at 11.30 a.m. Spent afternoon in reconnoitring old trenches in neighbourhood, to see necessary repairs required, stores, etc. Quiet evening. Splendid billet—bedroom to myself, feather bed and sheets, wash-stand; very lucky for once. First bed since leaving Boseghem four weeks ago. Good mess-room, fire and two arm-chairs. House kept by two middle-aged women, very kind, do anything; also little niece, aged eight, who speaks English well. She and I are good friends.

Jan. 5th.

Out with working party to repair trenches from 9.30 a.m. till 1.30 p.m. Lunch and letter-writing. Went up to — later to execute several shopping 2commissions. Had splendid crop first since — after patiently waiting one hour. Oh! these French hairdressers! One snip of the scissors every five minutes; one requires the patience of Job.

Went to pictures; pretty fair; and had dinner at the Lion d'Or. It seemed very quiet and deserted compared to my last visit, when the M.C.s were there. Back at 9 p.m., and to bed between the sheets.

Jan. 6th.

Out with working party, as per yesterday, from 10 a.m. to 1.30 p.m. Lunch 2 p.m. Inspection of B Co. by C.O. Me in command of company! Two-thirty, paid out to the men. Awful long job.

Jan. 7th.

Morning, 10 a.m. to 1.30 p.m., out with working party. H. called for few minutes, 2 p.m. Lecture on arms and care of rifles, etc., 4 p.m. Met H. at Lion d'Or in B. at 4.45 (splendid being able to do this). Tea, long chat and theatre at six o'clock. Panto., Alladin. Really tip-top, although men were disguised as girls. Plenty of fun and laughter. Sent in an application to-day for post as observer in R.F.C. Have great hopes. Life consists mainly of latter nowadays.

Jan. 8th.

Working party repairing trenches 9.30 to 1.30. Lovely morning. Two p.m., lecture in field on use of rifle—old as the hills (lecture); but I suppose they must work on the motto, "Anything to keep the time employed."

Sunday, Jan. 9th.

Marched to trenches (same place as Dec. 15). Beautiful day and everything quiet—not a day for war at all. On nearing the line the noise of guns and bursting shells broke on our ears, increasing in sound as we drew nearer, until we got as per usual in amongst them.

Had to go in single file at intervals up the infernal road. No one hit.

Got in the same old corner, and found to our relief the trenches had been built up again passably well after the bombardment of the night of Dec. 22.

Jan. 10th and 11th.

Contrary to expectations had two quiet days—of course, the usual few shells, but no great quantity. My platoon occupied the trench on left of company, instead of, as last time, close up on the right, 1000 yards from enemy.

Relieved at 8 p.m. on 11th, and we came back to the old keep

(— Farm). Everything very quiet all night, and enjoyed a good sleep on a stretcher in one of the cellars, despite the attentions of rats in plenty.

Quiet walk up to Headquarters for breakfast and back. Enemy began shelling roadway close by, and everything else within reach, at 11.20; still going on at time of writing, 12.45. When shall I be able to go up for lunch?

Got there intact.

Quiet day. Went back to front line at 7 p.m. for a further forty-eight hours. Quiet night.

Found in the morning that in addition to the usual bombs, grenades and shells we had a trench mortar opposite us, which kept lobbing big black objects over all day, burying men and knocking our trenches to pieces. There was not much else they could use on us now; but we gave them back two for every one we received, and at 2 p.m. we commenced a big "strafe" with rifle-grenades, bombs and mortars. It was good to see them bursting, and altogether we expended over 800 (!) in an hour.

We got all manner of things back, from a bullet to a 6-inch. The latter were falling 100 yards from the rear of our breastworks, and we could actually see them falling the last fifty feet or so.

All quiet by 4 p.m. Quiet night—far different to our expectations.

Each side shelling all day unceasingly, with the usual quota of bombs. We were relieved at 7.30 p.m., and came back in safety to —, after six more days of LIFE?

Very weary, and thankful for quiet and my valise.

Marched to a small village—seven miles, and found we had comfortable billets, and a mattress for the writer. Moving again to —, nine miles from here, to-morrow. HURRAH! We are (or should be) "out" for sixteen days.

Marched to — on the famous cobble-stones of France the

whole way. Poor feet! On arriving was delighted to find I had a cosy room with feather bed and a good mess 200 yards down the road. Spent the evening trying to get level with correspondence. Hope we shall stay here all the time. Shall spend most of my spare moments writing—one of my chief pleasures when out, especially now I've got a respectable pen!

Jan. 18th.

Slack day. Enjoyed the luxury of a "mess" and a fire. Spent a lot of time writing.

Jan. 19th.

My second birthday in the Army....

To-day's events, musketry and rifle drill, and shooting on a temporary range in afternoon. Lovely day—like spring.

Jan. 20th to 28th.

Detailed for course of bombing instruction; and between these dates I learn much concerning these nefarious love-tokens.

Jan. 28th to Feb. 14th.

Our period of "Rest." (Time spent out of the trenches is so miscalled in the Army!) It was extended for reasons known only to those in lofty positions, and we spent the time in performing all the evolutions of an infantry battalion in training, drill, manœuvres, etc. Of course, all this is very necessary after the sometimes enforced inactivity ofthe trenches, and helps to pull out the kinks; but it gets rather monotonous, and when we heard that we were off to the line again every one was glad.

Feb. 15th.

Said good-bye to our friends of the village and headed once more for the Land of Thrills. It took us three days, doing it in easy stages.

Feb. 18th.

Found ourselves in cellars in a much-ruined village just behind the line, viz. —. There were exciting events last night, before our arrival, a few enemy mines having gone "up," and as soon as we arrived we had to begin fatiguing, connecting up the craters with the front line.

(At this point the diary abruptly finishes; but the writer was kept busy from day to day in the routine manner, doing his turn in each line, with the usual "hate" progressing, but nothing of great importance happening. Long exposure to the severe weather sent him into hospital, thence home, invalided. The very day after he reported "nothing of great importance happening" many of his comrades fell in a gallant and desperate assault on the Hohenzollern Redoubt.)

CHAPTER XVIII

SAVING THE SOLDIER: DR. GRENFELL'S EXPERIENCE

[Leaving his great work in Labrador and Newfoundland, so that he might visit the front as a member of the Harvard Surgical Unit, Dr. Wilfred T. Grenfell spent three months in France as an army surgeon, and during a short stay in London related some of his experiences and indicated the marvellous advance that has been made in over-coming disease and saving our soldiers' lives. Not long ago in public, Field-Marshal Lord Grenfell said that when he and Dr. Grenfell went into large communities people did not say to Dr. Grenfell "Are you a cousin of Lord Grenfell?" They said to him (Lord Grenfell) "Are you a cousin of Dr. Wilfred Grenfell?" And he was very proud indeed to be able to say yes. Dr. Grenfell's two cousins, the twin brothers who were both captains in the 9th (Queen's Royal) Lancers, were killed in action, one of them, Capt. F. O. Grenfell, being the first of the recipients of the Victoria Cross granted for the present war. Two other cousins, the brothers Capt. the Hon. Julian Grenfell and Sec.-Lt. the Hon. G. W. Grenfell, sons of Lord Desborough, have also fallen in the war.]

I am on my way from France to Labrador, and I am really sorry to be out of khaki, though I never was in it before.

While I was in the thick of my work on the other side of the Atlantic I was invited to join the Harvard Surgical Unit at the front. I found it possible to do so, because I knew that in my temporary absence my work in Labrador and Newfoundland would be faithfully carried on by my friends and devoted helpers. So I came over and was attached to the Harvard Unit with the rank of major, and theexperiences I have gained as an Army surgeon will remain amongst the greatest and proudest of my life.

I have had the opportunity of seeing what the British Army is doing in many ways in this terrible war. I have been at many places, including the base at Boulogne, and many great battle-centres, such as Ypres, Bethune and Armentières. And I have been in the trenches, so that I have had full chances of seeing what is really

146

going on. It is hard, almost impossible, to find words in which to express admiration of the courage, endurance and humanity of the British troops in this terrible conflict.

All my life has been a roving one, ever since I took my degree as a doctor exactly thirty years ago. When I really began life I decided to look for some field of work where I could be useful. I went into the London Hospital, and very soon became intensely interested in the Royal National Mission to Deep Sea Fishermen. In those days the fishing vessels were all sail, and when a man was seriously injured he had to be transferred to some vessel that was carrying fish to Billingsgate, and then he was taken to the London Hospital. This state of things on the North Sea brought home to one the possibility of Christian men preaching the gospel of love and help; and men went out and largely brought about that wonderful revolution which we see to-day amongst North Sea fishermen.

I cannot help feeling that in the trenches, right along the line where the surgical men are working, there is just the same problem to deal with as we encountered in those early days of mission effort in the trawling fleets. Very great difficulties had to be overcome in performing operations in tiny mission hospital smacks on the open sea far from land; just as unusual obstacles have to be surmounted in treating wounded fighting men at the front to-day. The problem in the North Sea was to heal men's bodies, as well as to help them to take a higher view of life; and it seems to me that the problem at the front is just the same.

In dealing with the body there have been preventive developments which are little short of marvellous. The history of war is not the history of wounds, as a rule it has been the history of disease; and speaking as an unbiassed person I think that in this connection we are doing a perfectly magnificent work.

First of all, the troubles of the trench fighting have been the gas bacillus, which is an animal bacillus, and the tetanus bacillus. Both began operations in this war with terrible results, but now they have scarcely any effect.

It must be remembered that the soil in France and Flanders, where so much of the fighting has taken place, is highly cultivated, and is therefore splendid breeding-ground for these deadly bacilli. So much is this the case with tetanus that in the early stages of the war bits of uniform which have been driven into the body, however slightly, were infinitely more dangerous than serious wounds caused by clean shrapnel, for the cloth, by contact with the soil, had become infected with the bacillus. I have seen men with pieces of shrapnel left in their wounds and doing well, but a piece of uniform, sodden with the rich soil, was a very different thing.But so

147

wonderful has been the advance in the method of treating tetanus that to-day, if taken in time, such a thing as a fatal result is extremely improbable. Every soldier is so quickly and skilfully treated that danger practically does not exist.

The very terrible gas bacillus caused another very common disease, for the gas produced a kind of gangrene; yet now there is very little mortality indeed from this cause.

In the beginning, too, any number of men were lost from typhoid fever, but now typhoid is getting so rare that if a case occurs anywhere on the front it is known the same night at the French General Headquarters. That remark applies to the whole of our armies, and so rigid is the control which is kept over these matters that, on the day following the report, a searching local inquiry is held as to the cause of the disease.

At the front I saw men who came from all parts of the country where I have been working for the past twenty-five years— Canadians, Americans, and so on. And in passing just let me say that in connection with this war we are misjudging America because of the attitude which the President has taken. I have stayed with Mr. Wilson and with Mr. Roosevelt, and I know that the spirit of America is with us. It is because the whole spirit of the American people is with us that thirty-three doctors and thirty-six nurses— most of them giving up splendid practices—went out from America to the front, as the Harvard Unit, to help us. Just so the Chicago Unit, and many more Americans fighting in the ranks.

I have seen at the front men of all ages and of every rank in life—veterans who were a long way over the army age, and immature youths of sixteen or seventeen. The spirit of loyalty and the determination to do their bit made them go. Often enough a boyish patient would smile when I looked at the chart and asked him how old he really was. "Oh, that's my Army age," he would say, and go on smiling.

I was right round the trenches two weeks ago, and as that was early in March and the winter has been exceptionally bad, the conditions were intolerable. There is no anxiety, because everybody is sure that the line is strong; but the wet, mud and exposure make you think that the men will get pneumonia and bronchitis; yet what mostly happens is trench-foot. I have seen a lot of that in Labrador, where we call it frost-bite. It is not, however, the same, though it appears to be. I have travelled many times in Labrador in winter, when the thermometer has been twenty and thirty degrees below zero, and I have never had frost-bite except once in my life. That was when I was driving my dog-team over the ice. The ice broke and my dogs went into the sea. They shared a floe with me throughout an awful night, and my life was saved at the sacrifice of theirs. I have told that story in detail elsewhere, so I need not tell it now.

I saw 150 men from a Highland regiment with frost-bite, but that was quite exceptional, and was due to the phenomenal weather and the impossibility of relieving the men when their relief was due, because they were fighting continuously for over forty-eight hours.

There is another direction in which immense strides have been made, and that is with respect to vermin. At one time, at the beginning of the war, there were as many as 4000 men who had scabies, or itch, and were out of action for the time being; but you hardly see such a case now, because of the wonderful measures which are taken to keep the troops perfectly clean and fit.

Close behind the trenches immense vats have been placed to serve as baths for the men, and the happiest fellows I saw were those who were rolling and splashing in these hot baths, while their uniforms and clothing were being thoroughly cleansed in super-heated steam-chests and finished off with heavy hot irons.

Just as we got into one of these cleaning depots a Jack Johnson burst very near us, but nobody took the slightest notice of it, so accustomed does one become to the happenings of war. Five or six men were in each hot bath, and something like 2000 baths a day are given. The men become thoroughly clean personally, and their clothing also is perfectly freed from vermin and filth, and the troops look as happy as possible.

I was greatly struck by the coolness and courage of all who worked in these laundries, women as well as men, and I could not help thinking that if I stood one week of it I should be entitled to the D.S.O. Endless thousands of uniforms, socks and articles of underclothing are constantly dealt with in the manner I have described, and many of the workers are under artillery fire all the time.

In the treatment of bad wounds, too, there has been a very great advance, and for such cases as broken femurs such an ingenious device has been hit upon that you might well say that instead of putting a man into bed you put the bed on to the man. The R.A.M.C. is really doing its very best, and I shall go back to America feeling perfectly satisfied that the British soldier is getting all the attention that I could wish to have myself.

When the war began the surgeons did not know where to put the wounded, because of the varying fortunes of the fighting. Even Boulogne, Calais and Havre were not certain of safety, so that attending to the wounded and accommodating them was a precarious thing; but the temporary hospitals have been gradually replaced by stationary hospitals, the mobile makeshift has been

149

succeeded by the permanent institution, and so splendid and complete are our resources now that in one day the enormous total of 100,000 casualties could be dealt with by the R.A.M.C.

Casualty clearing-stations, field ambulances, advanced dressing-posts and fixed hospitals are about as perfect as they can be made; and so admirable are the arrangements that I saw one man who had been shot through the abdomen and was in hospital in less than an hour from the time he was wounded—which is almost quicker than you would do it in London.

A great many of the less seriously sick and wounded do not have to go to the base at all; at times one rest-camp was sending 80 per cent, straight back to the line, entirely new men; and, as they say in America, it would "tickle you to death" to see how these things are done.

If you count up the men who have been wounded and invalided from all causes you will find that there are still twice as many sick people as there are wounded; and the strange thing is that as there are more wounds there is less sickness, because directly a "push" comes the men don't think nearly as much about sickness as when there is nothing doing.

If you take 1000 persons in ordinary civil life you will find that there will always be 3·3 sick per 1000; but at the front the rate is not quite half as many—only 1·8 per 1000 men. It is a very strange thing, but I have met with a number of men who were always more or less sick in civil life, yet who got quite well again at the front. The trenches are the place for a change of air!

I am sure that after this war a very great many men will never go back to the civil life they were in before. They must have more life in the open air; and there can be no finer field for them than that glorious Canada which I know so well, with its boundless possibilities of harvests and material development.

One is impressed at the front with the apparent valuelessness of human life, and deeply impressed by the lavishness with which that life has been laid down by all ranks for King and country. This remark applies to every rank of life without exception, to the highest of the aristocracy as well as to the humblest private. And very remarkable, too, is the zeal and willingness to serve in quite subordinate positions of men who have had every advantage in life, particularly the University type.

I remember at one place, when we were sitting in the mess, a sergeant brought in a paper, which he handed to the colonel to read. It was a most elaborate scientific treatise on the body vermin that so greatly trouble our troops, and it was beautifully illustrated. In addition to that the paper showed the willing endurance of personal suffering for practical purposes that I for one should not have cared to undergo, for the sergeant had made himself thoroughly well acquainted with the effects of the visitation of the pests he described.

I was so much impressed by the performance that I said to the colonel, "Who is your sergeant?" and he replied, "Oh, he's the Professor of Entomology in the University of —!"

As I talk my mind takes me back to Labrador and its ice-bound coast, and I recall that when working through the ice-fields in our little mission ship, the *Strathcona*, or travelling in lonely regions with my dog-teams, I saw so many evidences of the eagerness of men out there to do their bit in this tremendous war. Almost to a man, when they heard that we were fighting, they wanted to come over. But at first in Labrador we got very little news, and when news did come it was not credited. "Oh," said the men, "don't you believe it. They've always got some scare on. They're going to put the price of fish up!" Fish, you know, is the greatest of all material things out in that vast and lonely land. But what happened when they knew that it was not a scare, but real war, and a fight for liberty and justice? Why, 1500 men of Labrador and Newfoundland went into the Navy alone, and these brave and splendid fellows crowded into the Army too. A thousand of them were in Gallipoli. And wherever they were they found their hard experience of the utmost worth. Our trappers soon learn the knack of getting a seal with the gun, though the seal only just pops his head through an ice-hole and the tiny target is the hardest of all things to see. But the trapper gets him—he seldom misses; and whenever a German puts his head out—well, he gets it too.

I have been in Labrador twenty-five years, and I am proud of the way in which my friends out there have done their duty at the front.

My own view of life is that one has to do one's duty in any place where one happens to be; and I know from what I have seen that our splendid fellows at the front have the same outlook. There are many, many soldiers out there who, with practically nothing to look forward to when the war is over, are sustained by one great thing, and that is the knowledge that they are doing their best.

I have mentioned Canada as a great place for receiving men who will be set free when the war is over. I have just seen the statement that Canada has gone prohibition from end to end, and that pleases me very much. I have spent thirty years amongst deep-sea fishermen and sailors as a medical missionary and a master mariner, and I have shared many dangers with them in the North Sea, out on the Labrador coast and elsewhere, but I have seen more sorrow and misery in the homes of our seafaring men through drink than I ever found in even small craft at sea.

All these things that I have spoken of come under the heading of practical religion and real Christianity, and rightly so. I do not believe in the Christian religion being negative; it is essential that you make it positive.

www.ingramcontent.com/pod-product-compliance
Lightning Source LLC
Chambersburg PA
CBHW011511170626
46810CB00009B/3326